Deadly Consequences

Deadly Consequences

The Zombie Murders

Robert E. Marx

Prominent Books

Writing: Robert E. Marx
Editing: Writer Services, LLC (WriterServices.net)
Cover Design & Book Layout: Writer Services, LLC

ISBN 10: 1-942389-17-5
ISBN 13: 978-1-942389-17-0

Prominent Books and the Prominent Books logo are Trademarks of Prominent Books, LLC

TABLE OF CONTENTS

DEDICATION

This book, as well as this series, is dedicated to the Profession of Oral and Maxillofacial Surgery. This 2018 year is its 100-year anniversary. History has now witnessed that, from its humble beginnings, this field has ascended to its established position and is an indispensable resource in modern healthcare.

CHAPTER 1
The Birth of a Zombie

The young man shivers as he walks down the long, chilly hallway; a reaction as much to the eerie silence as the temperature. It is two minutes after midnight, and the rest of Dade County Hospital has begun its transition from lazy Sunday to frenetic Monday, but down here, two floors below street level, it is as silent as a tomb … *literally*. The young man chuckles at his own joke, then pushes open the heavy double doors in front of him. The loud creaking sound cuts through the quiet like a warning, then his nostrils are assaulted by the smell of strong disinfectant. For a second, he considers turning around and marching right back to the elevator, then he shrugs the thought off and steps inside the morgue.

"Yo," he calls out with more bravado than he feels, "anybody home?" His voice bounces off the cold concrete walls and tiled floors of the morgue, then fades to nothingness.

"Over here…" replies a calm, somewhat gravelly baritone voice. "Just walk to your left by the scrub sinks, and you'll see a path between the gurneys."

The young man does as he's told and nearly gasps aloud when he sees the stainless steel gurneys, about thirty or so, organized into neat rows. They are covered with white-shrouded mounds of various sizes and shapes. Fighting the urge to run, Tyrone looks straight ahead and advances toward a large wooden desk. Behind it sits a stocky, seventy-ish black man, his grey head bent over a stack of paperwork. Next to him sits an old-fashioned gooseneck lamp, its light giving him a strange, almost other-worldly glow.

"Hey, I'm looking for Mr. Bland...?"

"Well, you found him," the man replies dryly, not bothering to look up from his work. "And you are?"

"Tyrone Chastain, your new intern."

"Oh, yes, you're the senior from Miami Jackson Senior High School. That's in Liberty City, right?"

"Yes, sir," Tyrone says, a note of pride entering his voice. "Graduating this year. You from Liberty City too?"

"Not anymore, but I still have some friends there." Bland gestures toward the chair in front of the desk. "Sit down, Tyrone."

As Tyrone steps forward, Chester Bland finally lifts his head to gaze upon the young man, his eyes registering slight surprise. "No, wait a minute," he says, and Tyrone stops moving. "Son, if you're going to be my intern, you're gonna have to wear your cap on straight. In my day, you wore your cap like that, you better be like Roy Campanella." Bland chuckles, then notes Tyrone's questioning stare and adds, "Catcher for the old Brooklyn Dodgers, and my own boyhood hero." He continues his scrutiny of the young man's appearance. "And pull up your pants. If you're gonna work around here, I don't want to see your ass crack or your underwear either. Understand?"

"Yes, sir," Tyrone says crisply as he straightens his hat and pulls up his oversized grey shorts. "Sorry, sir."

Bland looks the young man in the eye, searching for signs of mockery. Seeing none, he asks, "Did the human resources people tell you what your duties will be around here on the night shift?"

Tyrone gives him another blank look. "You mean the people that hired me?"

Seems like a nice enough kid, Bland thinks, *but maybe not too bright.* "Yes, those people."

"They said I'd be moving stretchers around and that they would have dead bodies on them." Tyrone's respectful tone does little to disguise his internal misgivings.

Bland now removes his glasses and smiles reassuringly at the young man. "That's right, son. You're not afraid of ghosts, are you?" A low chuckle escapes the triage chief's lips when he sees Tyrone's eyes go wide. "That's just a little morgue humor. Actually, it gets pretty lonely around here. It'll just be you and me most of the time, and sometimes it'll just be you."

Tyrone's eyes once again flick over the rows of gurneys as if sizing up a threat.

"A-alone with these stiffs?" he stutters.

Bland lifts his left eyebrow, a gesture he often uses to

emphasize an important point. "Yes, son, and if you're gonna work for Chester Bland, you're going to have respect for these dead folks. What are you, Tyrone—eighteen?"

"Uh, se-seventeen, sir."

"Okay, well, I was about your age when I started, and I never called them stiffs. We call them *the deceased*."

"The deceased," Tyrone repeated. "Got it."

"Okay, then, let's get right down to it. What we do here is receive the deceased from the general hospital wards, the ICU, and the emergency room. We record their intake information and arrange for their next destination." Bland meets Tyrone's eye. "That's where you come in. Most will go to our van out the door behind me and to the loading dock in the east parking lot. But some will be marked for the ME's office. You know what I mean by the ME's office, don't you?"

"Medical Examiner, right?" Tyrone grins. "I've seen 'CSI Miami'."

"That's right, son," Bland says with a smile. "Now, others will be picked up by the funeral home, some will go to a crematorium and—"

"Cream-a-what?"

"A crematorium, son. That's where they incinerate the deceased. You know, burn them into ashes."

"Okay, got that."

"Some will go to the pathology department for autopsy,"

Bland points in the direction of the morgue door, "which is just down the hall, and on rare occasions, a deceased will go to the tissue bank. Those we put at high priority once a donor consent is signed by the family, because there are some bones that must be collected within eighteen hours of the person's death." Bland suppresses a smile when he sees Tyrone shudder. "So you see why it's important to keep the paperwork and the bodies straight around here. A deceased goes to the wrong place, and it brings a whole world of trouble down on us." Bland picks up a clipboard. "Now, come over here, son, so I can walk you through this intake sheet. This is what you fill out when—"

Bland is interrupted by a creepy and, to Tyrone, unidentifiable sound. The young man twists around to look toward the gurneys.

"Aaaagh! Mr. Bland, Mr. Bland, look! She's alive!" He leaps up and darts around the old wooden desk, half-tripping over the thick black cord and knocking the gooseneck lamp over. He stands behind Chester Bland, shaking and pointing at one of the gurneys. The deceased has moved to a half-sitting position with knees raised and balanced on heels, bottom, and elbows. The white sheet has slipped to reveal the upper torso of a young white woman with long blonde hair. She is still in the low-cut shimmery blue dress she'd been wearing when she arrived in the emergency room five hours earlier from a drug overdose. Even from where he is standing, Tyrone can see that her eyes are open, and that may be the scariest thing of all.

"Well, son," Bland says, seemingly unruffled as he reaches over to right the lamp, "I guess it's time for your first lesson."

The old triage chief then stands up from the desk and grabs the clipboard with the intake sheet before moving toward the gurney. Along the way, he stops at a table and pulls a pair of blue rubber gloves from a half-empty box.

"Any time you touch a deceased, you need to wear these." Bland turns to see Tyrone still cowering behind the desk. He slowly straightens, and for a moment Bland thinks he's going to bolt. Instead, Tyrone takes a tentative step toward him.

Bland waits patiently as the young man walks over and pulls a pair of blue gloves over his shaking hands. "Now, son, what do you notice about this one?"

Tyrone stares down at the young woman, carefully avoiding her eyes as if afraid they might suck him in, then he blurts out the first thing that comes to mind. "Well, she's very pretty...." One look at Bland tells him this was not the response the triage chief was looking for. "Oh, okay, um, it looks like she is trying to sit up. And why are her eyes open?" Suddenly struck by a terrifying thought, he turns to Bland. "Can she see me?"

"No, she can't see you!" Bland shakes his head, though it's not the first time he's been asked that question. "She's dead. She's in this position and her eyes are open because she is in rigor mortis. I'll tell you, son, when I saw this happen for the first time, I was even more scared than you."

"Oh yeah? What is this rigor morbid thing?"

"Rigor *mortis* ... Son, I thought you said you watched 'CSI'."

Bland paused for a moment, trying to recall a conversation he'd had some years ago about the phenomenon. He'd never forget how Dr. Robert Merriweather had taken the time to explain it to him. Unfortunately, Bland could not recall much of the scientific detail. He looks at the still-shaky Tyrone and realizes the young man wouldn't be able to process it anyway. "Rigor mortis is what happens to a body between five and seventy-two hours after it dies. All the muscles contract—something to do with the calcium in the muscle cells—and because we have more muscles that bend us forward and those muscles are stronger than the ones that bend us backward, some deceased in rigor mortis end up in a sitting position like this." Bland points a blue-gloved finger toward the corpse. "See how her arms are bent at the elbows and her hands are clenched in a fist? Those muscles are contracted and stronger than the ones that straighten out the elbows and the fingers."

He turns to Tyrone, watching with satisfaction as the young man's expression turns from fear to curiosity.

"Cool, man, really cool."

"Speaking of cool, feel her skin."

Tyrone hesitantly follows Bland's instruction. "Wow, that's more than cool; it's almost *cold*."

"That's right. After a person dies, the body cools down, especially in this chilly old basement."

Tyrone nods in agreement and makes a mental note to bring a sweatshirt the next time he works. "But how did she die? She looks so young."

"She was young," Bland says, looking down at the clipboard. "Just twenty-two." He continues flipping through the sheets until he finds the "Cause of Death" section. "Says here it was a drug overdose—cocaine and heroin. It's everywhere these days. The news calls it 'the opium epidemic.'" He looks down at the young woman and shakes his head. "I call it a damn shame."

Using his pointer finger to guide the way, Bland skims the rest of the sheet. "Says here she was found slumped over in the bathroom of Club Princess on Miami Beach, her skin blue as the dress she's wearing. Her name is listed as 'Chrystal Pink'—obviously not her real one—which means she was probably a high-end hooker picking up clients on the strip in Miami Beach. She was DOA at the ER. Before you ask what DOA means, it means 'Dead on Arrival.'"

"Yes, I knew that one," Tyrone replies. "Where is she gonna go?"

"Chrystal will be sent to the ME's office, where all unnatural deaths—including those in which foul play is suspected—go."

Chester Bland is about to continue when one of the gurneys three rows away begins to shake and rattle. Tyrone takes a step closer to Bland as another rigor mortis event unfolds in front of them. This time, a young, athletic-looking black man jerks to a sitting position, exposing a bare, chiseled chest and ripped abdomen. A tattoo on the left arm faces the two observers, while his blank eyes stare straight ahead.

"Tyrone, let's go check this one out." Motioning for Tyrone to follow, Bland calmly walks over toward the gurney and once again looks down at the clipboard. "It's says here that his name is John Doe. That means they don't know his real name yet. What do you notice about him?"

"Well, he's got a real cool tattoo on his left arm." Tyrone pauses then tentatively places a gloved hand on John Doe's hand. "He also feels warmer than the girl did, and his knees are not bent like hers."

"That's very observant, Tyrone," Bland says encouragingly. "And yes, that is strange. Now, see if you can make out any writing on the tattoo. It might help the police find out his real name. Look for a gang insignia, a girlfriend or a team, something like that."

Tyrone moves in to get a closer look. "You're right, Mr. Bland! There is an 'S + B' on the top and 'HS' on the bottom."

"Let me see that." Chester Bland hands Tyrone the clipboard then leans over the deceased and attempts to twist the muscular left shoulder to directly view the tattoo. Tyrone stands a foot or so away, proud at having caught such a potentially important detail. When he sees the deceased's eyes open wider, he says nothing, thinking his own eyes are playing tricks on him in this creepy place.

Suddenly, the corpse's large hands reach up and grab Chester by the throat. His eyes bulging in terror and surprise, he pulls at the arms, trying to break free, but he is no match for the vise-like grip around his neck.

The clipboard falls from Tyrone's hand and clatters on the floor. He knows he should do something to help, but it feels like his body is made of cement. He watches helplessly as John Doe pivots to stand to the right of the gurney and dangles Chester Bland as easily as he would a doll.

"Yo, guys, this isn't funny," Tyrone blurts out. "I mean it, stop this shit right now!"

Chester Bland, his arms flailing wildly, manages a gasp in response, then Tyrone sees a frothy foam coming from the old man's mouth.

Suddenly, it hits Tyrone that this is no joke. This thing is alive, it is killing Bland, and if he doesn't leave, he is going to be next. He pushes through the gurneys, past the scrub sinks, and out the door. It isn't until he is running down the hall that he finds his voice. The words, "Help! There's a mother-fuckin' zombie down here!" echo down the desolate hall as he darts into the nearest stairwell.

Less than a minute after Tyrone's exit, Chester Bland succumbs to the relentless grip on his throat. Yet even as he hangs there, arms slack at his sides and swollen tongue protruding from his lips, the irony of the situation—that he is going to die in the morgue—is not lost on Chester. He finds himself less upset about dying than the fact that he will never understand what happened. *Well,* he thinks before losing consciousness, *ain't this a bitch.*

John Doe stares unblinkingly ahead as he releases his grip, allowing Chester Bland to plop onto the floor like a wet beach towel. Then, as if emerging from a long sleep, he looks around and surveys his location. He spots the red exit sign above the back door and begins moving toward it, not with the shuffling, jerky gait and outstretched arms of zombie lore, but with a straight, smooth stride. Still staring straight ahead, he deftly pushes several gurneys aside then pulls open the door and steps onto the concrete ramp of the loading dock. The east parking lot of the hospital is desolate with just a few parked cars. John Doe weaves his way among them then disappears into the balmy October night.

CHAPTER 2
A Zombie Earns a Reputation

The Chief Resident of the Trauma Service keeps one eye on the clock as he takes hurried bites of a dry vending machine sandwich. Across the table, his junior residents talk sports as they wolf down bags of pretzels and potato chips. Their shift started only three hours ago and already they've dealt with a ruptured spleen from an assault and an exploration of gunshot wounds to the abdomen and chest. Such things are not unexpected at a busy, four-teen-hundred-bed hospital, even at one a.m. on a Monday morning.

What they do not expect is a young man running down the main hallway, screaming, "A zombie, a zombie, a for real zombie!"

The three doctors drop their food and rush from the cafeteria just as the source of the screams—a tall, lanky African American teenager—rushes toward them. Behind him, a harried-looking nurse is trying, unsuccessfully, to stop him before he reaches the exit door.

"Whoa, fella," the Chief Resident says as he steps forward to block the young man's path. "What's going on? Stop, let us help you." Though the doctor's voice is calm, there is an underlying sternness that says he means business.

"I'm telling you, I saw a zombie," the youth blurts out, wild-eyed. "A *zombie!* Big dude, over seven feet tall. He's down in the basement right now, choking my boss!" With that, he tries to break away from the doctor, but the two junior residents quickly move to secure his arms.

The Chief Resident turns to the nurse. "Janice, get security." He then resumes in a gentler tone. "What's your name, fella? Did you come through crisis intervention?"

"It's Ty-Tyrone, and no, no it's nothing like that. I'm not crazy, man. Like I said, I came from the basement. That's where it is—a big fucking zombie. I tell you it's for real."

A moment later, Nurse Janice returns with two armed security guards who were making their rounds not far away. The older, stockier of the two is bearing the name badge Paul Castanza. He motions for the doctors to step back from the young man.

"We'll take it from here, doctors." He turns to Tyrone. "Now what's all this commotion about?"

"*Zombies* are what all this commotion's about," Tyrone says irately. "It's down there, right now, choking my boss! That's what I been trying to tell these doctors, but they ain't listening to me!"

Castanza nods patiently. If there's one thing he's learned in his twenty-four years on the job, it's that it never pays to fight crazy with crazy. "Well, *I'm* listening to you. Who is your boss, and where is he?"

"It's Mr. Bland, the old guy who works down in the place where they put all the stiffs, uh, I mean *deceased.*"

The Chief Resident draws back in surprise. "You mean the triage morgue?"

"Yeah, that's what he called it—the *triage morgue.* We thought it was rigor-something, but the guy got undead and attacked Mr. Bland. You all gotta do something!"

Castanza glances at his partner, a thin, thirty-something named Fred Johnston, as if to say *this is probably bullshit, but we'll check it out.* "Okay, Tyrone, show us exactly where this is happening."

"No way, brother, I ain't going down there again! No way!"

"Yes you are, young man. We'll protect you from this ... *zombie.*" Castanza hears his partner snicker and shoots him a look before turning back to Tyrone. "This better not be a false alarm, or you're in for a lot of trouble."

Leaving the astonished hospital staff in their wake, the two guards escort the reluctant young intern to the nearest elevator bank. As the elevator descends to the basement, Castanza notes Tyrone's darting eyes and shallow breathing. He might be crazy, the guard thinks, but he's not lying. A moment later, the steel doors open into the chilly, desolate hallway, and the three of them start moving toward the triage morgue, with each officer watching Tyrone to make sure he doesn't bolt.

When they reach the door to the morgue, Castanza motions for Tyrone to stay put, then he and his partner draw their guns and cautiously enter. After several silent moments, Castanza calls out in an almost sing-songy voice, "There's no one here, Tyrone...."

"Hey, I don't know, man," Tyrone whines as he steps into the room, "but I'm telling you the truth." He points a shaking finger toward an empty gurney in the area where Officer Johnston is investigating. "Look, the thing was lying right over there!"

Just then, Johnston's voice echoes throughout the morgue. "Paul! There's a guy on the floor over here!"

"Follow me," Castanza barks at Tyrone then quickly weaves around the other gurneys toward his partner. He stifles a gasp when he sees a black man with bulging eyes and protruding tongue lying next to the gurney. Though there's little doubt he's been strangled, Castanza squats down and peers at the neck area.

"Whoa!" Tyrone yells when he sees the body. "Is—is he dead?"

"Yeah, he's dead alright." Castanza narrows his eyes at Tyrone. "Are you sure this guy didn't fall off this gurney, and that's why it's empty?"

"No, man! That's Mr. Bland! I was talking to the dude a half hour ago."

Fred Johnston steps forward for a closer look. "He's right, Paul, it's Bland. I've seen him on my rounds." Johnston regularly checked out the basement hallways for the homeless guys who sometimes sneak in from the loading docks. More commonly, he stumbled upon some doctor-nurse tryst. But he always saw the genial man, now lying on the ground before him. "See, there's his employee badge clipped to his shirt." Johnston shakes his head sadly. "I don't know about any zombie, but there's definitely been a murder here."

Castanza sighs. There's no way this shift is ending on time. "Okay, get central security on the radio and tell 'em to call the cops." He turns to a terrified Tyrone. "C'mon, Tyrone. They're definitely gonna want to talk to you."

***

Some four blocks east of the hospital's east parking lot, beneath the concrete pillars and overpasses of I-95 and I-395 and hidden from view of passing motorists, lies an area about the size of a tennis court. In its dark recesses, two figures share a half-eaten meatball hero and a warm forty-ounce can of beer, both courtesy of a nearby trash can. Despite the dangers lurking about at this time of night, they are unafraid as they enjoy their feast thanks to a single vertical slit in the ten-foot chain-link fence surrounding their little kingdom. This is their secret doorway, the location of which is known only to them and a third resident whose whereabouts are currently unknown.

They made the place cozy enough with the discarded lawn chairs upon which they now sit, along with some old coolers, several flea-infested bed rolls, an old couch, and a mattress. There are also several cardboard boxes and even a camping tent, albeit with a few holes in the roof.

The three homeless have been together for years now and, aside from the occasional argument regarding their own perceived space within the enclave, have settled into an easy companionship.

Harvey, a scruffy, sixty-ish man with long, grey-streaked red hair, holds up a cardboard sign. "Hey Frank, whadd-aya think of this one?"

Frank, a fifty-eight-year-old black man with stark white hair, chuckles as he reads the words penned in black Sharpie: *Disabled Vietnam vet. No work and hungry. PLEASE HELP.*

"Oh man, you ain't no disabled vet. You got that bum leg falling off your motorcycle. Nam, my ass," he mutters. "You never got further than Fort Benning."

"Still a vet, ain't I?" Harvey retorts. "And Nam equals cash money. I'll bet I get more than you do working the same corner."

Frank takes in Harvey's dirty khaki shorts, worn sneakers and a brown tee shirt with a faded American eagle on the front. "Well, I sure hope you spend some of that money on new clothes. You look like shit."

The two men dissolve into laughter, then Frank adds, "'Sides, people don't go for that sob story stuff anymore; they want to see funny shit." He holds up his own sign that reads: *Ninjas captured my family—need money for karate lessons.*

Harvey is about to argue the point when they hear a rattling sound. They turn in the direction of their secret door to see a tattered woman in her late forties wrestling with an overloaded shopping cart. Dressed in a ragged and dirty dress, torn knee-highs, and stained silver shoes with well-worn heels, she bears no resemblance to the vivacious, attractive young woman she once was.

"Well, if it ain't Crazy Margaret!" Frank bellows. "We ain't seen you in a minute!"

"Yeah," Harvey adds, "where you been, woman?"

Margaret sucks her teeth. "If you two stop your bickerin' long enough to help me get my cart through, I might tell you."

The men quickly oblige, rolling back the fence enough for Margaret and her cart to enter. With surprising strength, she pushes it over the gravelly ground, knocking loose an assortment of bottles, cans and other urban treasures she picked up in her travels. Harvey and Fred hear the sound of glass breaking and hope it's not one of the bottles of liquor—some of them top-shelf—that Crazy Margaret always manages to score.

"Shit," she slurs, "help me pick this stuff up," then staggers back to watch the men do her bidding.

More than once, Harvey and Frank have speculated on how she gets her liquor—not like she can go up to her old fancy friends and ask them for a handout. Shit, Harvey and Fred still can't believe that a woman who can barely make a coherent sentence was once an accountant at one of Miami's top firms. Over the years, the two have taken bits and pieces from Crazy Margaret's rants and strung them together with local street gossip to create a rough sketch of her former life.

Unlike her compatriots, Crazy Margaret once upon a time enjoyed a rather cushy existence, with a husband, two daughters and lucrative corporate job. Apparently, she also liked her martinis with the after-work crowd, a habit she supplemented with the occasional line of cocaine. Somewhere along the way, that habit blossomed into full-fledged alcoholism and drug addiction, which led to the loss of her job and a very nasty divorce and custody battle, which she also lost. After flunking out of two rehab programs and alienating friends and family, Margaret quietly slipped into the world of the homeless. For the last decade or so, she's been a fixture on the streets, known simultaneously for her tenuous relationship with reality and her ability to get her hands on single malt Scotch. Neither Crazy Margaret nor the men remember exactly when they all "moved in" together, but it became a mutually beneficial arrangement, with Harvey and Frank sharing their space, listening to her rambles, and even offering her some measure of protection, while she in return has always happily shared her hooch with them.

As the men pick up the scattered remnants of her latest dumpster dive, Crazy Margaret digs her hand deep into the cart and lets out a squeal of delight.

"Looky what I got," she says, clutching two bottles of Jim Beam. "We're gonna party tonight."

The two men look at each other and grin—*pay dirt*. As the three head back to their lawn chairs, they notice a tall, muscular black man standing in the cut-out in the fence, which, in all the excitement, they had forgotten to roll back. Frank, the most able-bodied of them, approaches the intruder.

"Evenin', brother, can we help you?" The man doesn't answer, and, somewhat unnerved by his unblinking stare, Frank adds, "You want some of our whiskey?"

"Hey," Crazy Margaret slurs, arms waving in protest, "I work too hard for this stuff to give it to every Tom, Dick and Harry. Just send him on his way."

"Shush, now, Margaret," Frank says then turns back to the man, who continues to stare silently ahead as if he hasn't heard a word.

"You in some trouble, man?" Franks asks as he moves closer. "You need a place to hide out for a while? Don't mind Crazy Margaret. We can help you." When he again gets no response, Frank looks back at the other two and shrugs.

"You can lead a horse to water—" he begins, then lets out a gasp as he feels two enormous hands grip his shoulders. He tries to twist away, but it's as if he's trapped in a vise. "Hey, what the fu—?" He is cut off again when, with almost super-human strength, the intruder flings him into a pile of old hubcaps, refrigerators and mattress springs.

Dazed and in pain, Frank struggles to his knees only to be grabbed again, this time by the head. As the huge hands press against his temples, Frank is vaguely aware of Crazy Margaret's screams and Harvey jumping on his attacker's back, saying, "You're in trouble now, big boy. This Army Ranger has got you."

Damn fool, Frank thinks, then he slips into unconsciousness.

The intruder easily shrugs Harvey off and starts pounding Frank's head against one of the metal fence posts. Undaunted, Harvey launches another attack, this time brandishing a crowbar he found lying among the debris. He stops shorts when he sees the intruder drop Frank's limp, broken body to the ground.

"Son of a bitch!" Harvey screams as he raises the crowbar. Staring at him with wide, expressionless eyes, the intruder stops the crowbar with his left hand then grabs Harvey's long hair with his right. The last thing the homeless man sees is the weapon whipping down toward his face, then darkness.

A few feet away, Crazy Margaret crouches behind her shopping cart and watches as Harvey's lifeless body slides to the ground. "Please don't hurt me," she whimpers as the intruder turns in her direction. "I wo-won't tell anyone, I pro-promise."

He takes a few steps in her direction, and though it is only for a moment, it is the most lucid Crazy Margaret has been in years. Visions of her old life—her daughters, her husband, her lovely Coral Gables home—flash through her mind and then leave just as quickly.

I've already lost everything, she tells herself, *so what's it matter what this man does?* She closes her eyes and waits for the blow, then realizes the intruder has passed her and is slipping through the opening in the gate. As she watches him disappear into the night, she reaches for the bourbon and, with a shaking hand, raises it to her lips.

CHAPTER 3
Murder Scene Number 1

"Can't you go any faster?" Isabella Ruiz says impatiently. "It's not like you've never driven in the rain before."

It's nearly two a.m., and the unmarked black sedan is hovering just above the speed limit as it travels north on the nearly empty US-1 highway toward Dade County Hospital. In true Florida fashion, the previously clear skies abruptly opened up to release a torrential downpour.

Detective Andy Molinaro shoots an amused glance at his partner and live-in significant other. "What's the rush, Issy? The dead guy's not going anywhere."

Issy rolls her eyes. "Very funny. Now, what did the chief tell you?"

"Not much," he says as he presses down on the gas—a gesture of appeasement, "just that a man was murdered in the hospital morgue, and some hysterical kid is blaming it on zombies."

"'Scuse me?"

"Yeah, how's that for your first homicide?" He glances at her again. "I'll check out the scene, you interview the kid, alright? You up for this?"

Though on the surface, it's something he would ask any newbie detective, but in this case, it means a heck of a lot more.

"As ready as I'll ever be," Issy replies, sidestepping the deeper implications, "thanks to the relentless tutelage of your former partner. I think he's worried we'll do something to tarnish his record."

"Sounds like Gonzalez." Andy chuckles. "Retired from the job and still trying to control everything." He reaches over to squeeze her hand. "But he has always supported us."

It has been a year since Isabella resigned from her position as secretary to Dr. Robert Merriweather to enter the police academy. It was not an easy decision; she'd been working for Merriweather for years and had not only witnessed his rise to pre-eminence as an oral and maxillofacial surgeon and researcher, but liked to think she'd played some small part in it. They also had a close relationship that felt more like family than employer-employee. But after helping solve the brutal murder of Dr. Merriweather's mentor Dr. Jacobsen, Issy could not deny that she had both the passion and the skill for investigative work. Within weeks, she had applied to the police academy and gave Dr. Merriweather her notice. To assuage her guilt over abandoning him, she arranged for her twenty-year-old daughter Michelle to take her place.

Between her excellent physical condition and the knowledge she had absorbed over the years from her detective ex-husband, Issy soon exceeded everyone's expectations, including her own. But even stars at the Academy have to pay their dues, and Issy would have had to as well were it not for favors from several high-ranking detectives, including, ironically, her ex. Andy's former partner, Enrique Gonzalez, had also pulled some strings. Though forced into early retirement after suffering a serious heart attack during the Jacobsen investigation, the much-respected and beloved detective still had quite a bit of clout. He not only saved Issy years of walking a beat; he also managed to convince the chief to allow her to partner with Andy. Usually, romantic relationships within the squad are frowned upon, and partnering with significant others is a big no-no, but in their case, the chief agreed to make an exception.

While they are thrilled at the thought of working together, Andy and Issy also know that they are under much more pressure to solve cases. Indeed, rumblings and rumors about her meteoric rise have already been circulating—most of them involving some illicit affair Issy was allegedly having with some department mucky-muck. Issy sighs; it has been the one fly in the ointment, but in the scheme of things, she considers it a small price to pay.

"Issy, you know all eyes are on us," Andy says as if reading her thoughts, "especially with a sensationalized murder like this." He snorts. "A zombie running around killing people? I can see the headlines already."

"That's for sure," Issy says vaguely, already mentally rehearsing her questions for the murder witness.

"And remember, no one except the chief can know that we're anything more than partners. She was very clear on that. That means no chitchatting in the ladies room, okay?"

The truth of his words hit a nerve. "I get it, Andy," Issy says, squaring her shoulders. "I also know that women are more demanding of their female colleagues than they are of men. It's not just the police force; I saw it when I was working for Dr. Merriweather. Our female administrator was much harder on the two girl surgical assistants than the one guy assistant, even though they worked like dogs and he was MIA half the time." She shoots Andy a mischievous smile. "Just because I'm sleeping with you doesn't mean I'm going to cut you any slack, and just because I'm a rookie doesn't mean I'm going to just tag along."

Andy reaches for her hand again. "You never do, Issy, and that's what I love about you."

They pass the rest of the ride in companionable silence, then Andy pulls up under the canopy of the circular drive in front of the main entrance to the hospital. As they approach the door, a uniformed security guard steps out to greet them. Paul Castanza's eyes flick over the handsome, six-foot-three-inch detective with neatly combed salt and pepper hair and his attractive, raven-haired partner.

Only in Miami, he thinks, rolling his eyes. *These two look less like cops and more like models from a GQ photo shoot.*

"Detectives," he says, stepping forward with a meaty hand outstretched, "Paul Castanza, hospital security. We certainly have an interesting situation this evening."

"Nice to meet you," Molinaro says cordially as he shakes Castanza's hand. "Tell us what you got."

"The deceased's name is Chester Bland, a seventy-year-old African-American male and chief of the triage morgue here at the hospital. Approximate time of death, 12:30 a.m."

"And what about the kid claiming he saw zombies?"

"Ah yes, Tyrone Chastain. He's over at the trauma unit, conference room one. He's a bit spooked by all of this."

"I can imagine," Molinaro says dryly to indicate his skepticism about Tyrone's story. "Okay, Detective Ruiz, why don't you talk to Mr. Chastain. Mr. Castanza, you stay here and keep everyone away from the crime scene—that includes doctors, all staff, and especially anyone that looks like media." Castanza nods. "Put someone on the stairwell and block access to the elevators." Molinaro continues, "Your assistant can take me down to the morgue."

"You got it, Detective."

Just then, a tall, distinguished man with silver hair and a stern demeanor approaches them. "Hello, Detective Molinaro, is it? I was told you would be heading the investigation. I'm Edgar Vargas, CEO of the hospital."

Molinaro nods and accepts the man's manicured hand. Though it's just after two in the morning, Edgar Vargas is immaculately dressed in a two-thousand-dollar suit and clearly ready for the inevitable press conference.

"Hello, Mr. Vargas. I'm on my way to assess the crime

scene now. I'll personally update you on the situation as soon as we know anything. You can assist us by keeping this under wraps for now and providing a list of all your personnel on duty tonight."

As Andy heads down to the morgue to meet with the CSI team, Issy is walking into trauma conference room one. Most of the small space is taken up by a rectangular Formica table surrounded by eight card-table-type chairs. On one side is a Marlex board with some leftover teaching points having to do with sodium-potassium balance. On the other side are four old x-ray view boxes, one with its cover broken, indicative of their disuse due to a conversion to digital x-rays. In the far corner is a bolted down keyboard and computer screen used for medical records and viewing the digital x-rays and other imaging techniques of modern medicine.

In the middle of the table sits Tyrone Chastain, his cap once again turned backwards, as it was before Mr. Bland's scolding. Directly opposite him sits a thin, freckled, red-haired woman scribbling copious notes.

"Excuse me," Issy says, pulling out her detective's shield as she brusquely addresses the woman, "but who are you?"

The woman quickly stands and walks over to Issy with a small, almost timid smile. "Nice to meet you, Detective. I'm Clara Catherine Murphy, but please call me C.C." The smile deepens. "Everyone does."

"And what are you doing here, Ms. C.C.?"

"It's just C.C., and I'm interviewing this young man for the Miami Tribune."

"Well, *just* C.C., this is a homicide investigation. I must ask you to leave."

"Oh, I am so sorry, Detective, I didn't mean to break protocol." C.C. adopts a sheepish tone. "This is my first big story ... can't I just sit over there in the corner while you talk to him? I won't be any trouble."

Issy shoots her an incredulous look. "C.C., even a journalism intern knows you can't be present during an interview with a witness in an active homicide investigation. Now please go before I have you arrested."

Seemingly chastened, C.C. looks at the ground, but not before Issy catches the annoyed look on her face. Issy walks over to the door and catches Paul Castanza, who is posted nearby.

"Officer Castanza, please escort Ms. Murphy off the hospital premises. If she returns, have the uniforms arrest her for interfering with a police investigation."

"Nice to meet you, Detective," C.C. says sweetly as Castanza ushers her from the room.

Issy shoots her a disgusted look in response. "And, Officer Castanza, please make sure no other 'journalists' get in here."

As Castanza leads her towards the main entrance, C.C. Murphy makes several unsuccessful attempts at small talk.

"I better not see you around here again," he says before leaving her in the circular drive where Andy parked earlier.

She maintains her sweet smile until his back is turned, then quickly pulls her cell phone from her pocket to call her editor. Just then, the phone rings.

"Hey, Chief, I was just about to call you. I'm just leaving the hospital. The cops kicked me out right after my last text to you—"

"Forget about that; I just heard over the police wire that there was another murder close by. You know the homeless hangout under the I-95-I-395 overpass?"

"Yeah, what about it?"

"Two murders, and guess what. The lone survivor is talking about a black 'zombie.'"

"Holy shit, like what the kid was talking about at the hospital." C.C. looks in the direction of the overpass, quickly dismissing any fears she had about going to such an area alone. "I'm on my way—will keep you posted."

Back in trauma conference room one, Issy sits in the seat formerly occupied by C.C. Murphy. "You're Tyrone Chastain, right?"

"Yes, ma'am," the young man replies. He looks exhausted.

"I'm Detective Ruiz," she says gently, "but you can call me Issy."

Tyrone nods and respectfully takes off his hat.

"Okay, Tyrone, why don't you tell me what you saw here tonight."

"This zombie sat up on the gurney thing," Tyrone blurts out, suddenly animated. "Mr. Bland and I thought he was still dead, but you know zombies are never really dead. Then when Mr. Bland leaned over to read the tattoo on the zombie's arm, the zombie grabbed him by the neck and choked him."

Issy sighs inwardly, not quite able to believe what she is hearing or that this is her first homicide.

"Can you describe the zombie's tattoo?"

"I don't know, man. It had a dragon on it and some letters, SB or ST something and HS. That's all I can remember. I got the hell out of there before more zombies came to life."

"Right, and what did the zombie look like?"

"A big dude, seven feet tall or more, with really big eyes. He didn't blink at all. It was creepy. I should've known he was a zombie."

As Issy tries to separate fact from fiction, Andy leaves the crime scene in the CSI team's capable hands and ascends the two floors to enter the controlled chaos of the emergency room. It seems everywhere he looks, there are patients moaning, doctors shouting out orders, nurses scurrying about, and patients' families trying to get someone to answer their questions. Molinaro flags down Edgar Vargas and tells him he needs information on a John Doe, medical record number 40201945422, who was pronounced dead in the ER three hours earlier.

Vargas leads him past the cubicles with electronic monitors,

IV poles, and cabinets full of basic medical items to an unused patient bay in the back corner of the emergency room. He then pages Dr. Vince Hagy, one of the emergency room physicians. Within minutes, an exhausted-looking thirty-something man in scrubs shows up.

Holding up an ER chart, Vargas begins. "Dr. Hagy, you pronounced this John Doe dead at eleven p.m., right?"

"According to my entry in the record, I did."

"What was the cause of death?"

"It was busy, let me look at my notes. Oh yeah, I remember him. Probably a drug overdose. People found him lying on a curb about two blocks from here. They dropped him off at triage."

"His ER chart says he was brought in around nine-thirty," Molinaro interjects, "but no one saw him until eleven when you pronounced him dead. Is that your routine here?"

"Listen, Detective, there was a rap concert at the stadium a mile away. We were flooded with drunks with injuries, gunshot wounds, knife wounds and, excuse my language, a whole shitload of drug overdoses. And that was in addition to the usual bedlam in here."

Molinaro holds up a hand. "Okay, Doctor, I get it. How did you know he was dead?"

"No pulse, no detectable breath sounds, no blood pressure."

"Did you do an EKG or an EEG?"

"No, there is none on the chart."

"Did you draw blood for an alcohol level or a tox screen?"

"No, he was taken to the morgue right away. The ME's office will do that. Listen, Detective, he was dead by my clinical exam. There was a family of five that came in from a nasty car crash at the same time. We were understaffed from the perspective of both doctors and nurses. We saved the mother and two of the three kids. Had we done more with John Doe, we would have lost one of the other kids. We did the best with what we had."

In the awkward silence that follows, CEO Vargas jumps in. "Dr. Hagy, you only need to let me know when you need more people. We would have gotten more doctors, more nurses and whatever else you need rather than have you cut corners. That's not what our mission at this hospital is all about."

"Gentlemen, I'll let you discuss your corrective action plan later," Molinaro says, barely able to hide his annoyance. "Right now, we need to find out who and where this John Doe is, dead or alive."

A few minutes later, Andy and Issy meet up at the hospital's main entrance to compare notes. Just then, Frank Sinatra's rendition of "I Did It My Way" starts blasting from his suit jacket. He quickly retrieves the cell phone from his pocket.

"Yes, Chief."

"You and Ruiz still at the hospital?"

"Yeah, we're—"

"We'll talk about it later. Right now, I need you to beat it over to the I-95-I-395 underpass. There're reports of another so-called zombie murder. The foot patrol officers are there now but so is some nosey reporter who was caught talking to a witness. Get her the hell out of there. You understand?"

"On the way, Chief."

As he ends the call and tucks the phone back in his pocket, Molinaro feels an unpleasant tightening in his gut. From the looks of it, he and Issy are headed straight into a storm, one that has little to do with the Miami weather.

CHAPTER 4
Bevo St. Claire's Big Tumor

At first glance, the crimes seem unrelated. Chester Bland was strangled in his workplace; the two unidentified men at the second scene were bludgeoned to death, one by a crowbar, the other against a fence post in a known hideaway for the homeless. But no one could deny the obvious connections—both crimes were committed within minutes of each other and less than a mile of each other. Neither had any ascertainable motive, and both were committed with a force that appeared impossible by human hands. And then there was the biggest connection of all—the alleged perpetrator, first described by Tyrone Chastain and then a ranting loon who self-identified as "Crazy Margaret," as a large, athletic man in an almost trancelike state, who stared blankly ahead, did not speak and struck without provocation but with merciless brutality.

After running off C.C. Murphy, the two detectives attempt to interview Crazy Margaret, only to come away with an expletive-laced string of phrases that have nothing to do with the situation at hand. She also screamed for Harvey and Frank, which at least gave the other cops a starting place for possible victims' names.

By the time Andy and Issy leave the scene, the rain is long gone, and the sun is just starting to peek over the horizon. They'd like nothing more than to go home and catch up on some much needed sleep, but with a triple homicide, that's little more than a pipe dream. Instead, at eight a.m., they are at Cutler Ridge Police Station, standing before the desk of Chief Jennifer Russell. An attractive if rather stern-looking black woman in her late forties, Russell has always been a highly-respected member of the force, both for her integrity and her exemplary work. She also has a reputation of always being in control and not taking any crap from anyone, including her detectives.

"Well, well," she says, folding her hands in front of her on the desk, "a big black muscular zombie is murdering people with his bare hands. You two really stepped in it, didn't you?"

As usual, Chief Russell cuts right through the bullshit— one of the many reasons Molinaro loves working with her. Though she has been chief for only five years, the two have known each other for ten, back when Molinaro, then an FBI agent, served with her on a joint drug task force. They hit it off right away, and when he later learned that "Jenny," as he used to call her, became the first black female chief in her squad, he was genuinely thrilled for her. The respect was mutual, and when he later joined the Miami Police department, Russell immediately hired him.

"Yes, ma'am," Molinaro says now, his lackluster response a combination of exhaustion and complete bewilderment about the case.

"Well, I doubt the ME's office is going to find anything to help you. Now, how are you going to go about finding who and what John Doe really is?"

Molinaro clears his throat. "Well, we plan to review the computer database for missing persons, escaped felons that fit the description, all ERs in Miami and canvas the neighborhood around where this guy was found before being taken to Dade County Hospital."

Judging from Russell's expression, she is singularly unimpressed. She turns to Isabella. "What about you, Ruiz, any bright ideas?"

"Yes, as a matter of fact, I think we should run these findings by my former boss."

Russell raises an eyebrow. "The dentist?"

"Actually, Chief, Dr. Merriweather is an oral and maxillofacial surgeon and a leader in stem cell research. That man has forgotten more about medical conditions, drugs, and how the body works than most people ever know." She smiles. "And, let's just say he specializes in highly irregular situations."

After a brief silence, Russell says, "I like it, Ruiz. You think outside the box, and it sounds like Merriweather does too. You and Andy have a lot of work to do, so I suggest you get to it."

Chief Russell smiles as she watches the two detectives exit her office. Against her better judgment, she allowed the couple to partner, but now it seems the arrangement may work out after all. Suddenly, a shadow crosses Russell's face as she remembers her own fiancée who was killed in a shootout with a drug gang during the Mariela Boat Lift fiasco. That was back in the days of the Carter Administration, and though she has dated her fair share (and then some) of men since then, none have ever held a candle to her Charles. She closes her eyes momentarily to stop the threatening tears, a practice she's perfected over the years. If she hadn't, she would have quit the force long ago. A ringing telephone interrupts her reverie, and Russell returns to the mundane reality of administrative police work.

✳✳✳

While the two detectives are meeting with Chief Russell, Dr. Merriweather arrives at his Dade County South Office, having just completed morning teaching rounds with the residents and fellows in his oral and maxillofacial surgery program. He sighs when he opens the door and sees the impossibly large stack of printed emails and medical forms on his large cherry wood desk.

"Mishy, what've we got going this afternoon?"

A moment later, the click-click of heels is followed by the sight of his secretary. She is carrying another bundle of printed emails and a notepad containing twenty or more phone messages, most requesting a return call.

"Hey, Dr. M," she says smiling cheerily, "and to answer your question, we have a whole lot going on."

At twenty years old, Michele Ruiz is a stunning younger version of her mother, Issy. A statuesque brunette with big green eyes and shapely legs that seem to go on forever, Mishy, as she is called, is everyone's dream girl.

"First up is this message from a Mr. Steve Turner; I marked it as urgent. He asked that you call him today because he's leaving for Haiti tomorrow."

"Okay, let's try to reach him now. I still have a few minutes before Drs. Glanville and Strong arrive to discuss our surgical case."

"Got it," she says with a wink then heads to her own office. A moment later, she buzzes him to announce that Steve Turner is on the line. "Oh, and Drs. Glanville and Strong just walked in."

"Great, they're early. They can hear this too. Please show them in, and then you can transfer the call here."

A moment later, Mishy returns followed by Dr. Glanville, his fellow in tumor and reconstructive surgery, and Dr. Strong, the chief resident. The two take seats across from his desk, and although they both offer cordial greetings to Merriweather, their eyes remain glued to Mishy. No surprise there. She's dressed in a black, tight-fitting pencil skirt with a white silky blouse opened to show her ample cleavage. Together, the two pieces perfectly accentuate her already provocative hour-glass figure.

Merriweather clears his throat then looks pointedly at the wedding ring on Glanville's left hand. "Shall we begin?"

"Yes, Dr. Merriweather," Strong replies while the red-faced Glanville just nods.

"Okay then. Thanks, Mishy, you can transfer the call now."

She slips away, and a moment later, the phone on his desk rings.

"Mr. Turner," he says after pressing the speaker button, "this is Dr. Robert Merriweather, can I help you?"

"Thanks for calling me back, doctor. I was afraid you wouldn't."

"You're quite welcome. I actually have two of my colleagues here with me, is that okay?"

"Yes, no problem. I'm calling because I saw that show about the little girl who had the twelve-pound tumor of the tongue and how it was so huge it had pushed down her neck and was laying on her chest. You guys are amazing. She practically looked normal afterwards."

"Thank you. It was quite a challenge to remove the tumor, but I'm proud to say that she has been back home for three years now and has continued to grow normally."

"That's great news. I'm actually calling about a similar situation. I'm a fireman from just outside Toledo, and I've been doing mission trips down in Haiti for more than ten years now. On my last trip, I came across a man living in the remote hills—I'd say he's in his late twenties—with a huge tumor in his lower jaw. His tribe and local village have ostracized him because voodoo is a large part of their culture, and they feel he's possessed. The thing is so big he can hardly eat, and between that and the villagers not helping him, he's basically starving. I know I'm asking a lot, but do you think you can help him? I took him to Port Au Prince to see a group of plastic surgeons doing cleft lip surgeries on another mission. They brushed us off. Said it was cancer and probably terminal. Do *you* think he has cancer? I emailed some pictures this morning."

"You did? Great. Let me see if I can find them in my pile."

He shuffles through the stack of emails for a moment. "Okay, here they are..." He hands them to Glanville and Strong, who both nod at him. "Well, Mr. Turner, I can tell you that this tumor is certainly very big, but it's not cancer. I'll bet it has been slowly growing for more than ten years, just like the Vietnamese girl's tumor did."

"That's right! He said he first noticed it when he was about twelve years old."

"I suspect that this is actually an ameloblastoma."

Drs. Glanville and Strong both nod their heads in agreement.

"An amelo-*what*?"

"It's called an ameloblastoma. It arises from the cells that otherwise form the white surface of your teeth. It's a tumor we're very familiar with and have seen some over four pounds. From the look of your pictures, this one is at least twice that."

"Wow, do you think you can help this guy?"

"Yes, I think we can, but it won't be easy. Does your mission have any funds to support his medical care?"

"That's just it—we don't." Turner sighs. "I know I'm asking a lot, but we're desperate."

"That's alright, Mr. Turner, we're happy to waive our fee for the surgery. The hospital uses a lot of its own resources—probably totaling around $40,000—but I think we can get some donations for him. We also have some money left in our charity account to pull it off."

Merriweather looks up to see Glanville and Dr. Strong high-fiving each other and grinning; they're already pumped about being involved in such a challenging case with the chief.

"Oh, God bless you," Mr. Turner says, "all of you. That is just fantastic."

"Hold on there, Mr. Turner! You'll have to help us. You need to get this man—by the way, what is his name?"

"It's Bevo St. Claire."

"Does Mr. St. Claire have a passport?"

"Yes, sir, we just got him one last week."

"Okay, great. Plan to get him and yourself on a plane to Miami this Thursday. I'll ask American Airlines to comp his ticket. They've done that before for us if it's truly a special case. I'll use my frequent flyer miles to get your ticket. We'll schedule his arrival for the evening so that his appearance doesn't disturb the families of the other patients here. How does that sound?"

"Terrific, terrific, it's more than I had hoped for. Thanks a million."

"Mr. Turner, we've gotta get over to the operating room now. Coincidentally, we're removing an ameloblastoma about the size of a tennis ball from a basketball player with aspirations for a career in the NBA. I have your email and phone number. My secretary will email you the tickets. We gotta go now. See you Thursday."

Turning to Glanville and Strong, Dr. Merriweather asks, "What are you two grinning about?"

"Wow, look at the size of that tumor," Strong says, pointing to the photo. "Only an ameloblastoma could get that big."

Merriweather shakes his head. "Now you sound like those misguided plastic surgeons. Remember, that tongue tumor in the girl from Vietnam was a schwannoma—a nerve tumor. You know that some benign bone tumors and benign salivary gland tumors can get that large too. The common thread is neglect or lack of access to the timely quality of care we tend to take for granted here in the US. Now, if you want to be involved in this case, schedule Mr. St. Claire for a CT scan when he comes in as well as a complete metabolic panel and blood screening. I'll bet he's protein deficient and probably more."

"Got it," Glanville says just as Mishy re-enters the office with more paperwork. The two young doctors stand to leave, their eyes now looking everywhere *except* his secretary. Merriweather might have thought it was funny if not for the uncomfortable conversation he was about to have.

"You have invitations to speak in Australia, Saudi Arabia and India," Mishy says, "and look at all these emails from other doctors asking for advice. How are you going to get to them all?"

"Only with your help, Mishy," Merriweather says, eyeing her. "But first, I want you to close the door and sit down."

"Sure, Dr. M. What's up?"

With a sigh, he says, "Mishy, just because Sharon Stone is my fantasy doesn't mean you should be auditioning for a remake of Basic Instinct."

"Dr. M, are you coming on to me?" she says saucily.

"Don't be funny with me, Mishy, this is serious. I've known you since you were ten years old, and you've grown into a beautiful young woman, just like your mother."

"So what's the problem?"

"The problem is, well … the way you dress is an invitation for problems. This is a professional office, and I need you to do me a big favor and dress less provocatively."

Mishy looks down at her outfit. "Dr. M, all the girls my age dress like this."

"Perhaps, but not at work." He sighs again. "Look, our residency program has several young men, most of them married, who work long hours and are under significant stress. The temptations on them to stray are great, and even though you may not think you're encouraging them, the revealing nature of your clothes does just that. We also have two female residents, and we don't want to create a climate where they might resent you. So I'm asking you to tone it down a bit, not as your boss, but as a friend to both you and your mom. Will you do that for me?"

"Of course, and I'm sorry. I really like working here, but is it okay to date the single guys?"

He pauses. "Yes, as long as I don't have to hear about it and you don't let it interfere with your work, or theirs."

CHAPTER 5
One Zombie—Two Zombies

Tuesday morning finds Captain Jennifer Russell at her desk with a steaming cup of coffee in her right hand and a frown on her face. Before her is the early edition of the Miami Tribune, which, like every morning, was waiting for her when she arrived fifteen minutes earlier. It is a well-known fact that the captain refuses to take her news online.

"'Zombie' Murders Befuddle Police."

Russell shakes her head as she takes in the header, then the byline below it. As always, C.C. Murphy has wasted no time in her efforts at self-aggrandizement and stirring up fear in the public eye, usually at the Department's expense. It is an ongoing campaign.

Just then, the wood and frosted glass door bearing the chief's name and title slowly opens. The receiving clerk tentatively peeks her head in and looks around as if to gauge her boss' mood.

"Mayor Ecchavaria on the phone for you, Chief."

"I know what he wants. I'll take it on my private line. Thanks."

Russell waits for the door to close, then with a sigh picks up the phone. "Morning, sir," she says formally, though they've known each other socially for years. It's the tone she uses when she's about to have a conversation she doesn't wish to have.

Sure enough, the mayor foregoes the usual pleasantries and gets right down to business.

"I assume you've see this morning's Tribune...?"

"Looking at it right now, Mr. Mayor."

"Then I don't need to tell you that we have to get a handle on this situation before we have a full-scale panic on our hands." He snorts. "People watch 'The Walking Dead' and the 'Twilight' series and think there really are things that go bump in the night. Throw in this reporter's nonsense, and it's like a match to a flame."

"I know, sir," Russell replies, "and it has top priority. As of yet, we don't have many leads—all initial assessments point to one guy with mental and/or physical issues—but I've assigned my two best detectives to the case, and I'll be supervising it personally."

"I'm sure you will, Jennifer," Mayor Ecchavaria replies in a slightly softer tone. "And I just want to let you know you have the full support of my office behind you. Anything you need for your investigation, you let me know. That includes more detectives; I can pull them from other precincts."

"Thank you, sir. That won't be necessary for now, but I'll hold you to that offer if I need it."

"Okay, just keep me informed," he says, then hangs up.

Russell sits there for a moment with the phone still clutched in her hand, debating whether to call Molinaro and Ruiz. That's what the mayor would have her do—pass the pressure on to them—but the former detective in her knows she needs to let them do their work. Like she'd told Ecchavaria, they are her two best detectives. She brings the coffee to her lips and decides she'll wait until she's finished her second cup before checking in with Molinaro.

"Probably some nut escaped from a mental ward," she mutters to herself.

That theory would be shattered as soon as the sun goes down.

***

That night, just after dark, Esteban "Pepito" Garcia is working the cars that pull up in front of Liberty City's most well-known crack house. This popular, highly lucrative establishment is also an unfortunate remnant of the area's checkered past. In 1980, Liberty City gained national attention after the death of a black man named Arthur McDuffie and the subsequent acquittal of several white officers believed responsible. Four days of rioting ensued, leading to several deaths, more than eight-hundred arrests, and eighty million dollars in damage. It gained further notoriety as the main source of gifted black athletes were recruited by the University of Miami football coach Howard Schnellenberger; he would later be known for plucking youths from the inner city and developing them into the dominant college football teams of the 80s and early 90s. In recent years, Liberty City has faded back into obscurity. The racial tensions of the past have subsided, and the desolate inner city image mostly reversed, yet part of the area remains a hub for gang activity, including the drug trade.

Pepito sees a familiar old Ford crawling past the house and steps toward it.

"Yo, Pepito, you got good stuff tonight?"

Pepito eyes the thin, young black man inside. "Sure do, brother, top o' da line."

"I need two bags."

"That's ninety for you."

Without another word, the man brings his hand up to the window and positions it low against the outside of the car door, four twenties and a ten folded between his pointer and middle fingers. Pepito looks around quickly then steps up and swiftly exchanges the requested bags for the money. The man slowly drives away as if he's casually cruising through the neighborhood. The whole transaction took less than thirty seconds.

The next customer, a white guy with a scruffy beard and a wedding ring, is followed by men in expensive suits, blue-collar workers, and a few well-to-do housewives, all jonesing for the particular white cocaine or heroin

Pepito is known for carrying. In between, Pepito services the occasional pedestrian who surreptitiously hands over their money as they pass him by. Yes, it is a busy night, and Pepito is very good at his job.

Even Pepito's trade, however, is no match for the higher level transactions taking place in the house behind him. Leo Lewis, or "Leo the Leopard" as he's known on the streets, is the most successful drug dealer in recent Miami history—no small feat in a city whose trade spawned the term "Cocaine Cowboys" in the 80s. Leo's almost comical, self-proclaimed status as an "entrepreneur" and "purveyor of services to the public" pisses law enforcement off almost as much as his elusiveness.

Pepito pauses in his work when he sees two potential new customers walking up. One is a twenty-ish man with sandy blond hair hanging over his ears and a beard-mustache combo. His large, six-foot-three-inch frame is dressed in a white sleeveless T-shirt and plaid shorts. The other, a muscular black man of the same age, stands even taller—six-foot-seven or so—and is wearing brown shorts and an orange jersey with the number 52 on it. It is a popular jersey commemorating the career of All-American and All-Pro linebacker Ray Lewis from the "U" and the Baltimore Ravens, respectively.

"You guys want to do business with Pepito?"

The two men don't answer; they just look down at the smaller Pepito with a catatonic, unblinking stare.

"If not," he jerks his head toward the house, "I'll take you inside to see my boss. He has anything you want."

When he still doesn't receive a reply, Pepito shrugs and struts past the unkempt lawn toward the dilapidated one-story home where the Leopard conducts his business. When he reaches the doorway, he glances back to see that the two men are following him.

Pepito suppresses a shiver. After a lifetime working these streets, nothing much surprises or scares him, but these dudes are *strange*. It is with a sense of relief that he steps into the safety of the house.

It is business as usual at the Leopard's. The skunkish scent of marijuana mingled with sweat, old furniture, and something sweet and unidentifiable drapes the room like a heavy curtain. To his left, a black man in his fifties leans back into an old, tattered brown sofa with a leisurely smile on his face. On each side of him, a scantily-clad girl several years his junior is slumped over in a state of drug-induced drowsiness. Pepito smirks at the telltale traces of white dust just under their nostrils.

Yup ... Just business as usual....

In a corner to his right, five guys—two white, two Hispanic, and one black—are engaged in an animated game of craps. Each man has either a cigarette or one of the Leopard's "special blend" joints clamped between his lips. Each intensely focuses on every role of the dice, then, depending on the outcome, lets the expletives or cheers fly.

Straight ahead, at a card table at the far end of the room, a thin, light-skinned black man in his early thirties holds court. A mane of dreadlocks flows past his shoulders; a light scruff covers his chin. Dressed in khaki shorts and a sleeveless shirt bearing his gold and black trademark pattern, the Leopard sits with one thin leg casually flung out like a man at leisure. Shrewd, beady eyes dart this way and that, belying the relaxed posture. Leo is famous for a short temper, a collection of knives and guns, and an enthusiasm for using them. To his right sits his "banker" and one of the few people Leo trusts.

Customers entering the home would approach the table to give Leo their order and pay the banker. Only then would one of the other employees retrieve the product from one of the back bedrooms. Anyone not following this protocol will be refused service; those who argue the point are risking their lives as well.

Leo's eyes flick from Pepito to the odd pair that followed him inside. "You two gonna stand in the doorway all night, or are you here to do business?"

Without a word, the two big men step forward, their unblinking stares now aimed straight at Leo.

The banker leans in and whispers, "Yo, these two look familiar to you?"

Leo shakes his head.

"Well, I know them from somewhere, and it's nowhere good. Can't you see there's something wrong with these motherfuckers?"

Leo runs a hand across his unshaven face. If he listened every time the banker got nervous, he'd never make a sale.

"Welcome to the Leopard's den," he says with a magnanimous grin. "You want rocks, crystals, powder, a smoke, brownies? Whatever it is, we have it."

When the two continue to stare unfazed at him, Leo glances at Pepito. The drug dealer just shrugs.

"Or maybe my man already fixed you up outside?"

Another strained silence follows, and Leo is just about to have them removed when Jasper, the shooter for the craps game, hands the dice to another player and walks up behind the pair. Smiling broadly, he reaches up and places a hand on each man's broad shoulder, then inserts his head between them.

"Don't be shy, boys. Tell Jasper what you need."

It isn't the first time Jasper has helped facilitate a transaction on Leo's behalf, and his success has earned him a standing invitation to hang at the house and even the occasional free fix.

As if awakened by Jasper's touch, the blonde man slowly turns and, with a low growl, lifts Jasper off the ground. A tense moment follows, then Jasper, the smile frozen on his face, flies through the air, straight for the card table.

Quick as a flash, Leo leaps to his feet and pulls a ten-inch knife from a sheath at his waist. But before he can wield the blade at anyone, the black man with the number 52 jersey steps forward and grabs Leo's wrist. A second later, his other hand wraps around the drug dealer's neck. Just then, Leo's wide eyes meet the cold stare of his assailant. His last thought before his neck snaps is that he should have listened to the banker. There is an audible crack, then the sound of his discarded body hitting the floor.

The room quickly descends into bedlam. The four remaining craps players split up, with two running for the door and the other two throwing themselves behind a huge, worn armchair. In the kitchen, Leo's employees slip out through windows and back sliders into the balmy evening. Even the two nearly unconscious young women on the couch manage to lock arms with their male companion and stumble toward the door. Fresh screams ring through the air as "52's" blond partner beats poor Jasper around the face and head with a heavy glass ashtray. The sound, coupled with the crunch of bone, seems to awaken Pepito, who has been standing frozen in the middle of the room.

Pepito gasps when he sees his boss slumped against the wall in a sitting position, his head down, dreadlocks covering his face like a shroud. Leo the Leopard is obviously dead. The banker is nowhere to be seen, but Pepito sees the mass of bloody pulp in the blonde man's grip and recognizes it as Jasper. He tries to run, but his legs feel cemented to the floor.

Suddenly, the two men turn and head directly for him. *This is it,* he thinks, unable to believe that of all the dangers he encountered on the job, two freaky dudes would be what did him in. He closes his eyes and waits for the pain. He feels nothing but the sensation of the blonde brushing against him as the two head for the door. Suddenly, he recalls the headline he saw on Local 10 news that morning.

"The zombies," he whispers hoarsely. "We've been hit by the motherfuckin' zombies."

***

Fifteen minutes away, Michelle Ruiz pulls into the lot of her Coconut Grove apartment. LA Fitness was even more crowded than usual, so she forwent her usual shower and headed home still dressed in workout clothes.

She walks in the front door and closes it behind her, making sure as always to secure the deadbolt, then pulls off her headband and shakes out her long, raven black hair. As she heads straight back toward the bedroom, stripping off articles of sweaty spandex, Michelle is completely unaware of the man peering at her from the living room closet.

She steps into the bathroom to turn on the shower, then into the bedroom to finish undressing. The phone on the nightstand is blinking with missed voicemails, and as she bends over to grab it, she hears a creaking sound from behind her. She straightens and looks around, then just as quickly dismisses it as part of the faint cacophony constantly playing in the background in the old building.

Michele stifles yawns through messages from her dry cleaner and her dentist, reminding of her of clothes to be picked up and an upcoming tooth cleaning, and a telemarketer offering a free carpet cleaning. She's about to hang up when she realizes there is one more message.

Michele's face splits into a grin when she hears Luke Young outlining the plans for her twenty-first birthday celebration the following evening: an elegant dinner at The Depot—the very fancy, very pricey Coral Cables restaurant—followed by an hour of paintball with some friends.

Michelle laughs, delighted. Only Luke would come up with the idea of bringing together such very different evenings. It was this kind of quirkiness that first attracted her to Dr. Merriweather's second-year resident in the first place.

She's still smiling as she finishes undressing, then she returns to the now steamy bathroom.

The man waits a few seconds, then exits the closet and heads toward the bathroom. When he reaches the door, he pauses to slip off his shirt and shoes, then listens to the sound of the water splashing against Michele's body. He quietly pushes the door just enough so that he can see her voluptuous form silhouetted through the steamed shower door. There is no turning back now. He struggles to quietly remove his shorts over a heated and throbbing erection, then slips into the bathroom and whips open the shower door.

Michele shrieks as the hand grabs her right shoulder and presses her forward. Another hand tightly clenches her left hip, and before she can react, the man forcibly enters her from behind. Stunned by the sudden, powerful onslaught, she places a hand on the shower wall as the intruder continues to thrust deep inside her. She hears soft moaning and is slightly aghast to realize it is coming from her. Her assailant grips her even tighter now and quickens his pace as the warm water splashes against their bodies. She reaches an orgasm and shutters uncontrollably, triggering a guttural sound from the man's throat as he explodes inside her. He releases his grip on her shoulder, and the two slump to the floor, breathing heavily. When she is able, Michele twists around to face her assailant.

"Luke, you dog, you're lucky I don't accuse you of rape!" she gasps, still trying to catch her breath. "Not exactly what I had in mind when I gave you the key to my place."

"But—but did you like it?" he sputters, unable to gauge her tone.

"Of course I did, you dumb jerk. That was as intense as I can ever remember."

She slowly stands and turns off the water, then holds a hand out to Luke. Smiling, he accepts the gesture and, once on his feet, presses his lips gently to hers. The two quickly towel off then stumble, exhausted, toward her bedroom.

Chapter 6
Hospital Rounds

Wednesday morning finds Dr. Merriweather on morning rounds at the Level I Ryder Trauma Center at the Dade County Main Hospital—the very same hospital where Chester Bland met his demise just three days ago. Normally, Merriweather rounds at the Dade County South branch, but today he is filling in for Drs. Brewster and Samanka, who are presenting lectures at the American Trauma Society.

The residents assigned to Ryder are both excited and nervous to have the Chairman there, for Merriweather is known for asking detailed questions and keeping those who seem unprepared on the hot seat. Fortunately, they were given enough warning to formulate their presentations on each patient.

"Okay, I'm impressed," Merriweather says after rounds are over, eliciting a sigh of relief from more than one resident. "It seems Dr. Brewster and Dr. Samanka have whipped you into shape. Do we have anyone in the ICU?"

"Yes, one," a thirtyish woman with short, blond hair replies, "an apparent assault victim. He came into the trauma center late last night, and neurosurgery admitted him to the neuro ICU. The police came by to speak with him, but he's intubated and in a coma."

Merriweather gives her a curt nod. "Okay, let's go see him."

They take the elevator to the third floor, where the fourteen-bed intensive care unit devoted to brain and spinal cord injuries is located. They find their patient lying in Bed 7 with a breathing tube taped to the left corner of his mouth and a ventilator breathing a sixty percent oxygen/air mixture down the tube into his lungs. He is unresponsive to their presence. He has intravenous fluid lines in each arm and another line in an artery in his left wrist. He is bandaged about the face and head. At his bedside, a young, slight Hispanic man sits staring in morbid fascination at all the tubes, machines, and screens.

Dr. Merriweather nods at the young man then steps forward to read the patient's name off his hospital bracelet. From the looks of things, Jasper Wiggins had a very rough night.

He turns back to the visitor. "I'm Dr. Merriweather. And you are...?"

The man's eyes flick from Merriweather to the five residents behind him as if debating whether to give his name. "Pepito," he says after a beat, "Pepito Garcia."

"And are you a relative of Mr. Wiggins?"

Pepito shrugs. "I'm his friend. He got no relatives."

"Do you know how he got injured?"

"Sure do. Two zombies beat his ass. Same ones who killed the Leopard ... my ... er ... boss."

Merriweather hears someone inhale behind him, and although he doesn't turn around, he knows the residents are exchanging knowing glances. These so-called zombies have been all anyone could talk about since Chester Bland's murder a few nights ago. Garcia may be his only chance to hear an eyewitness account.

"You saw these zombies, Mr. Garcia?"

"Yeah, man." Pepito's eyes widen at the memory. "Two big ones. They don't talk. They just growl and choke and beat people. They must be the ones from the newspaper."

Merriweather nods. The Tribune's story has certainly fanned the flames. "And what did these 'zombies' do to Mr. Wiggins?"

"The white zombie beat him with Leo's ashtray, right on the face." Pepito pauses. "The black one got my boss."

"I see...."

"Doc, is he gonna be alright?"

"I don't know yet, Mr. Garcia. I'll need to examine him and talk it over with the neurosurgeons." Merriweather notes the man's questioning look and adds, "The brain doctors. Now I'm going to have to ask you to wait behind this curtain while I examine your friend's injuries."

Pepito quickly stands and moves out of the area, only too happy to avoid seeing more gory evidence of the attack. Merriweather draws the curtains, pulls on some gloves and gingerly removes the bandages to reveal a truly grue-some sight. The bashed-in eye sockets, nose, and upper jaw make Jasper Wiggins look anything but human. Frac-tured bone segments are protruding through the skin of his face, and there is a clear liquid slowly oozing from the deepest fractured segment on the right side.

Dr. Merriweather immediately focuses on the right eye, which is hanging like a deflated balloon out of the pulver-ized eye socket. He also notices a laceration in the back part of the eye where the retina is located.

Dr. Merriweather calls for the ICU charge nurse.

"When did this man get up here?" he asks, alarm creeping into his voice.

"Just an hour ago," the nurse replies, then explains that Jasper lay at the crime scene for several hours with the other victims. When they realized he was still alive, he was rushed to the Ryder Trauma Center and intubated. It took several more hours to stabilize him. "He almost died, you know."

Merriweather nodded. "Has neurosurgery seen him yet?"

"No, but I expect them to come along anytime now. Why?"

"We need to get this man into surgery today. We need to know if he is neurologically stable and if they need to do any procedures together with us."

Dr. Merriweather pulls open the curtain to find Pepito waiting patiently. "Mr. Garcia, did your friend say he could see after his beating?"

"Yes, but only out of his left eye. He said I was ugly." Pepito pauses to gain control of his voice. "He always says that."

Merriweather gives him a sympathetic look. "Thank you, that's important to know."

He then turns to his residents and fires off some hard questions.

"Okay, can anybody tell me what that clear fluid flowing from the wound on the right side is?"

"Is it vitreous humor from the eye?" answers Dr. Montel, the chief resident.

"A good observation about the eye, but no. Vitreous humor is thick and gelatinous, like raw egg whites. This is clear and watery. It represents cerebrospinal fluid, CSF."

"Is that why you want to talk with neurosurgery?" Montel asks. "Do you want them to close the dura to stop the leak?"

"No, the best way to stop the leak is to fix the fractures and stabilize the bone. The lacerated dura will then heal by itself."

Priscilla, an intern visiting from the University of North Carolina Dental School, asks, "Excuse me, Dr. Merriweather, can you explain what the dura is?"

"Of course, Priscilla. It's the protective covering of the brain. It contains the cerebrospinal fluid that cushions the brain as we move our head back and forth. The name dura is short for *dura mater*, which means 'tough mother' in Latin."

Merriweather's gaze lands on Luke Young, who's standing directly behind Priscilla. The resident is usually on the ball, but this morning he seems oddly distracted.

"Dr. Young, you look a bit tired. Were you on call last night?"

"No, sir, I just didn't get much sleep."

"You're a single guy with no small kids," Merriweather says sternly, "and you weren't on call. I hope you're tired because you were studying all night, not out partying with some girl. Are you alert enough to discuss the risk and concern regarding Mr. Wiggins' cerebrospinal fluid leak?"

"I'm sorry, sir, and believe me, I wasn't out partying," Dr. Young replies, a hot flush creeping across his face as he turns toward the patient. "I think Mr. Wiggins is at risk for meningitis, so we need to be sure he's given high doses of antibiotics of the penicillin type."

"Very good," Merriweather replies wryly. "Now think how much better you'd be if you were fully awake."

Merriweather ignores the good-natured snickers of the others and peers curiously at Luke. Odd that the second-year resident would look so uncomfortable. It's not like he's the first resident to be called out in front of his colleagues.

"I'm sure you'll be fully awake," he continues, "when your anesthesiology rotation begins next Monday. When I visit Dr. Saltzman at the Pain Clinic tomorrow, I'll ask him to accept you for a special rotation on his pain research service."

"Th—thank you, Dr. Merriweather," Luke stammers.

"You're welcome. I know pain control is your interest. Do well with Dr. Saltzman. He's an old friend of mine."

Merriweather turns back to the others and the case at hand. "Our greatest concern here is the right eye, which, clearly, Mr. Wiggins will never see out of again. The left eye looks swollen, but thanks to Mr. Garcia, we have reason to believe he can see. Now, can anyone tell me how the right eye, which is not salvageable, places the left eye at risk for blindness?"

There is a momentary silence, then Dr. Montel responds, "Holy shit! Sympathetic ophthalmia, right?"

"Right! Now, who can tell me what sympathetic ophthalmia is and why we should remove his non-seeing right eye soon?"

The residents look at each other hesitantly, each waiting for someone to stick their neck out. Dr. Montel once again takes the lead.

"Well, it's not that the left eye will go blind 'in sympathy' for the right eye," he says, making air quotes. "It's not related to the sympathetic nervous system either. As I understand it, it's caused when the proteins from the retina and vitreous humor leak out of one eye and get into the bloodstream. These proteins, which have been shielded from the immune system since birth, are now recognized as foreign by the immune system, which builds up antibodies to them. These antibodies then attack the retina and vitreous humor of the good eye and can blind that eye too."

Merriweather nods approvingly. "Very good, Dr. Montel. Indeed, like a vaccine that produces antibodies to destroy certain viruses and bacteria, the antibodies stimulated by the leaked out protein of the injured eye will then attack the good eye, causing total blindness. To prevent this, removing the hopeless eye is necessary."

Dr. Merriweather then instructs his residents to get clearance from the neurosurgery team and add Jasper Wiggins to the add-on schedule for surgery later today.

CHAPTER 7

The Investigation Begins: A Third Zombie Appears

That evening, a tired but pleased Dr. Merriweather returns to his office after completing Jasper Wiggins' surgery. During the intense five-hour operation, he and his team removed the right eye and repositioned all the fractured bones in Wiggins' face, then stabilized each bone segment with titanium plates and screws. Already, the man's face has returned to an almost recognizable, albeit very swollen, form. It will be several weeks before they know whether the removal of his right eye prevents blindness in his left, but Merriweather is hopeful.

As he walks in, he is surprised to see Mishy still there.

"It's after six," he says. "Shouldn't you be getting ready for your birthday celebration?"

"Hey, Dr. M. Yes, I should be, but just as I was leaving, my mom and Andy came to see you—something about a case—and I stayed to chat with them. They're waiting in your office. Besides…" she gestures to the vase of roses on her desk, "I had to thank you for the flowers. You're a sweetie." Michele kisses Dr. Merriweather on the cheek.

Merriweather draws back, eyebrow raised. "Me, a sweetie? There's one I haven't heard in a while. Now, get out of here, go enjoy your birthday."

"I certainly will," she says mischievously, already picking up her purse.

He waits until she has her hand on the door, then says, "Oh, by the way, don't keep Dr. Young out too late."

Mishy turns around and gives him a curious look. "How did you know he was coming out for my birthday?"

"Just a wild guess."

Mishy laughs, thinking the residents were chatting about their paintball plans. "See you tomorrow, Dr. M, and thanks again."

She closes the door behind her, leaving Merriweather to wonder whether his theory about his secretary and one of his most gifted residents is true. Even if it is, he has more pressing concerns at the moment, like what Issy and Molinaro are doing in his office. As he walks toward the door, he hears snippets of conversation—one that includes the word "zombies". Crazy as he thinks this is, he cannot deny the curiosity that has taken hold of his mind.

"Issy, Andy, what're you two doing here?" he booms and is immediately greeted with a hug and a kiss by his former secretary and a firm handshake from her partner, who, in the past year, has also become a close friend. "Kisses from two beautiful women, it seems this is my lucky day. Now, what can I do for you?"

Dr. Merriweather takes his seat behind the desk. "Mishy said this is a serious visit, and from the look on your faces, it seems she's right."

"I'm afraid it is, Chief," she says, using the term of endearment from her days as his secretary. "We need your help."

"Am I correct in assuming this has to do with the so-called zombie murders?" he asks, unable to keep the mocking tone from his voice.

"Yes," Andy replies, "unfortunately it does."

"Oh come on, guys. You're not falling for all the fear-mongering by the media...?"

"Of course not," Issy says, "but Andy and I think there may be some medical problem that's making these two seem like zombies."

Merriweather raises an eyebrow at her. "There are *two* of them? From what I understand, one perpetrator killed Chester Bland." As he thought of the triage morgue chief, Merriweather flashed back to his days harvesting bone for the tissue bank. He and Chester spent many a night talking about the old baseball greats—Duke Snider, Ernie Banks, Willie Mays, Hank Aaron. Chester was also excellent at that job, and his presence would be sorely missed at Dade County Hospital.

"Well, Chief, there are now two zombies—the African-American man who allegedly killed Bland, and a white guy who apparently travels with him. In fact, it was the white zombie who beat Jasper Wiggins to within an inch of his life while his partner was killing some drug dealer in the same room. Neither appears to have any physical infirmity, so we're hoping you can tell us what, if anything, can turn young men into zombies."

"I sure can," Merriweather quips. "It's young women. It's happened to all of us."

Issy rolls her eyes at him. The Chief has always joked after a successful surgery; it's his way of releasing the pent-up tension, but what they need now is not his questionable sense of humor but his talent for thinking outside the box.

"Very funny, Chief, but can you please be serious?"

"I thought it was funny." Dr. Merriweather chuckles softly. "Actually, there are some psychiatric and medical conditions that cause zombie-like behavior, as do some of the drugs that treat those conditions. Sleep medications are a consideration as well, and when you throw in street drugs, well, anything is possible."

"Any suggestions on where we can start?" Andy asks.

"Yes, start with psychiatric conditions. Go over to the Dade County Mental Health Institute and inquire about young men treated for severe schizophrenia or Cortad's syndrome. It has a specific medical ICD-9 code of 297.1, which now, due to our following the European politicians, is ICD-10 code F22 and—"

Issy sees the look of growing frustration on her partner's face and politely holds up a hand. "Chief, I don't mean to be rude, but we're getting pressure to solve this case yesterday. Can you tell us what this Cortad's syndrome is? I never heard of it while I was working here."

Merriweather smiles. "Of course. Cortad's is also known as walking corpse syndrome and—"

"Okay, now we're getting somewhere," Andy says. "Every witness has described the perps as walking around like the dead. No emotion, no talking, no responding when spoken to. Just blank stares followed by brutal attacks."

Now it is Merriweather's turn to interject. "Hold on, Andy. Walking corpse syndrome has never been associated with any violent behavior whatsoever. The syndrome is more of a personal crisis—some feel that only one part of their body is dead, while others feel that most of their body is dead. Only a very small percentage of sufferers believe they are actually deceased. Besides, Cortad's syndrome is very rare. It would be unlikely to see two individuals with it at the same time, unless…"

"Unless what, Chief?" Issy asks. When her former boss pauses like this, he is usually on the verge of some break-through.

"Unless they are being treated in a mental health clinic." He taps a finger to his chin. "Indeed, you two need to look into the mental health clinic at Dade County Hospital. All the murders took place close by, didn't they?" The detectives nod in unison. "While you're there, be sure to query the doctors about schizophrenics and split personality patients. Those psychiatric diagnoses are noted for bizarre and sometimes violent behavior if not controlled with medications. And, as I mentioned earlier, some of the medications used to treat them dissociate brain function, resulting in that 'zombie-like' behavior of staring into space and the slow steady walk. Thorazine in particular is known for these types of side effects and is commonly prescribed for schizophrenics."

Molinaro looks up from the pad he's been scribbling on. "Thanks, Doc, that's a great start. But what about the street drugs you mentioned...?"

"...And any new legitimate drugs out on the market?" Issy adds.

Andy nods, grateful for her background in the medical field.

Merriweather pauses for a moment. "Well, actually, I'm going to Dr. Jake Saltzman's research lab tomorrow."

"Dr. Saltzman!" Issy exclaims with a smile. "How is he?"

Of all Merriweather's colleagues Issy had gotten to know while working for him, Jake Saltzman remains one of her favorites. He and Merriweather had met as residents in their respective disciplines—anesthesiology and oral and maxillofacial surgery—and though Jake Saltzman has since become an internationally known pain management specialist, he is still the same down-to-earth guy of his youth.

"He's doing fine, better than fine, and he'll be happy to know you asked about him. When I go there tomorrow, I'll pick his brain about your case; no one knows more about medications and drugs that affect the brain than old Jake. In the meantime, you two see what you can learn over at the mental health institute. Also..." He taps his chin again. "...You might want to look into drug rehab centers. Often times there's at least one person with information on combination drugs and is willing to snitch."

"Thanks, Chief," Issy says as she snaps her notebook closed. "We hesitated to get you involved…"

"Not a problem," Merriweather replies, waving away her apology, "but hold up a minute. Have you considered post-traumatic stress disorder? Go to any VA hospital, and you'll see plenty of veterans returning from the Middle East with it. Some of these cases can be quite alarming."

Merriweather then recounts to them his own military days, during which he took courses in battlefield medicine. The accounts of what was called "Shell Shock" and "Battle Field Fatigue" in the World War II and Vietnam eras described soldiers aimlessly wandering around the battlefield not knowing where or who they were. For many, these symptoms continued long after they returned home.

"You might be on to something here," Andy blurts out. "Issy, didn't the witnesses say that at least one of the suspects had a tattoo on his left arm?" At Issy's nod of agreement, he adds, "It could be a corps or platoon insignia."

"Well," Issy says, rising from her chair, "we certainly have a lot of work to do." She smiles at Robert. "Thanks to you, our investigation will be much more focused now."

"You're very welcome. I just hope the information I gave you doesn't lead to a bunch of wild goose chases."

***

Two hours later, as Dr. Merriweather is finishing the hellacious tasks associated with electronic medical records, three young men open the door to the Miami River Diner. Located just one mile southeast of Miami Dade County Hospital, the diner has been a beloved local institution for more than fifty years. The original décor, including red-cushioned stools at the counter and red-padded booths, has remained unchanged; the antique jukebox in the corner harkens back to an earlier, more innocent time.

"Sorry, boys," a gravelly voice calls out, "we're closing up for the night."

The three do not leave but instead quietly approach the counter. Behind it, a fifty-something man in a white apron and T-shirt with the name Ralphie sewn over the pocket mops the floor. Ralph Mathers, the owner of the Miami River, is as much a fixture in the neighborhood as the diner itself. He has worked there in one capacity or another for most of his life, first as a busboy, then a waiter, then a short order cook, and finally bought the place two decades ago. Much to his wife's dismay, Ralphie still works there six days a week, and although he loves most of his customers, he's also had to deal with more than a few troublemakers.

Ralph stops mopping and, for the first time, takes a good look at them. Two tall, young black men in their early twenties stare blankly back at him, as does the sandy-haired white guy standing in between them. Each is well over six feet tall and has the muscular, athletic build of a professional athlete.

"Seriously, guys, there's nothing I can do for you. All the food is locked away and…" Ralphie holds up his hands. "…If you have something else in mind, all the money is in the safe, which can only be opened electronically tomorrow morning."

The three young men continue to stare straight ahead as if they haven't heard a word.

"Hey George," Ralphie calls out, "can you come here for a minute?"

A moment later, a stocky, dark-haired man in his forties emerges from the kitchen, broom in hand. George Peabody, the Miami River's cook for the past fifteen years, is also a community treasure, best-known for his shrimp and grits.

"What's up, boss?"

"Can you tell me what's up with these guys?"

George glances at the three strangers, then back at Ralphie, who shrugs.

"Are you guys high or something?" George says as he takes a step closer.

No response. Ralphie and George exchange puzzled looks while their uninvited guests continue to stare straight ahead, as if engaging them in an eerie, silent standoff. The cook notices that each of the three young men has the same tattoo on his left arm.

He waits another moment or two then steps out from behind the counter, still clutching the broom.

"Alright," he says as he approaches the blonde man, "this has gone on long enough." Slowly, he waves his free hand in front of the blonde man's face.

"I don't know, Ralphie," he begins, "maybe we should call—"

Just then, as if jolted from a deep sleep, the young man grabs the cook by the shoulders and throws him on top of the counter. The broom falls from his hand and clangs to the ground.

George screams as much from anger as from pain as the left side of his body crashes into the marble. He recovers quickly then bounds off the counter and manages to retrieve the broom. Swinging it wildly, he catches the bulkier of the other two men just above his left cheek bone. The blow snaps the broomstick in two, yet George manages to get in another swing, this time aiming the shorter, jagged half at the blonde, opening up a small cut above his left eye.

"Gotcha, you sonofabitch."

He is still celebrating this small victory when he is grabbed around the throat by one of the others. The last thing George hears before his neck snaps is Ralphie's blood-curdling screams.

In the coming days, the brutal deaths of Ralphie Mathers and George Peabody would shake the city of Miami to its core. Though countless reporters, bloggers and "citizen journalists" covered the tragedy, C.C. Murphy would be catapulted to instant celebrity. She has always relied on her trusty police scanner to scoop the competition, but it never paid off like this.

Since her days as a cub reporter, C.C. has prided herself on not allowing emotions to get in the way of her job. Still, even this consummate opportunist has trouble keeping her breakfast down when she walks into the diner the morning after the murders. The scene is somehow even more macabre than the others with large amounts of blood, brain and other human tissue mingled with marble, broken glass and uprooted stools. George Peabody lies slumped on the floor in a bloody heap while Ralph Mather's nearly decapitated body was flung like a ragdoll across the counter. Within minutes, the buzz at the crime scene is that this is the work of the so-called zombies who've been ravaging the city.

The only thing untouched by the carnage is a large framed photo of a spectacular Miami sunset. It gives C.C. Murphy an idea that makes her forget all about her squeamishness. Her four-part series, *Zombies in Paradise*, would be the definitive source on the spate of murders, and a major thorn in the side of the Miami Police Department.

CHAPTER 8
The VA Blues

Issy Ruiz stifles a yawn as Andy pulls up to the main entrance of Dade County Mental Health Institute. It's Thursday, the start of their fourth full day working the zombie murders, but to her it might as well be a month. Little sleep and few leads in the case have led to exhaustion and testiness that no amount of coffee can cure. Issy should know; it's barely eight a.m., and she is already on her third cup. Her next yawn ends in a sigh.

"Told you homicide was no joke," Andy says with a sideways glance.

"I'm not expecting a joke," she replies wearily, "but some progress would be nice. You said it yourself, a lot is riding on this case."

Andy grunts in response. Captain Russell made it very clear, if he and Issy want to remain partners, they need to tie up this case quickly and with a nice little bow.

The two fall silent as they exit the car and walk toward the entrance, each praying this trip will yield some valuable information. The four-story building is fairly well-kept from the outside, but as they walk through the door, they immediately notice the peeling, dingy green paint on the walls, missing floor tiles, and the hastily scrawled "Out of Service" sign on one of the two elevators.

Ahead of them is a large reception desk, but before they can make their way to it, they are intercepted by a pleasant-faced, somewhat chubby woman in her forties with rosy cheeks and neatly combed short brown hair. She introduces herself as Carol Witek, the charge nurse, and asks what she can help them with.

As they pull out their detective shields, Andy introduces himself and his partner.

"The Director is expecting us."

"Oh, yes, Detective Ruiz," Carol says cheerily to Issy, "I spoke with you earlier. Follow me."

The woman makes small talk about traffic and the weather as she escorts them to the only working elevator. They step inside, then she presses the number four. The door slowly closes behind them, and the claustrophobic steel box begins its slow, jerky climb.

"The Director's office is located on the fourth floor," she explains, "as are most of our resident patients' rooms."

When the elevator door opens, Andy and Issy are struck with the musty smell of unwashed bodies mingled with stale food and urine. It's one of those unmistakable odors that fills your nostrils and, Issy thinks ruefully, clings to your clothes.

The solemn scene that greets them is even more disturbing.

Several individuals shuffle along the corridors, their eyes fixed at some invisible point in front of them. Clearly, they are suffering with the illnesses and/or side effects of medications Dr. Merriweather mentioned; their behavior also bears a striking resemblance to those of the "zombies" suspected in the recent killings.

To their right, a man is conversing with the wall twelve inches in front of him, his mutterings unintelligible to, and ignored by, others. Behind him, an elderly gray-haired woman strapped to her chair gestures with her hands while repeatedly uttering, "Now you got nothing, you bum," over and over again. Others seem to be higher functioning, chatting or playing checkers with their fellow patients, while still others sit motionless with a blank expression, presumably reliving past events, real or imagined, in their lives.

Despite the despair of the surroundings, no one seems especially agitated, and they are certainly not threatening. Most greet Andy and Issy's escort with a smile or a loud, "Good morning, Nurse Carol."

Never breaking stride, she responds to each by name and with a friendly smile. Two more turns down the corridor, and they arrive at an office with "Dr. Avery Birnbaum, Chief of Psychiatry" on the door. Carol raps on it twice, then gently pushes it open to reveal a small room dominated by a large oak desk. Behind it sits a portly man in his sixties with thinning gray hair and piercing blue eyes.

"Detectives," Dr. Birnbaum says with a warm smile and an outstretched hand, "welcome." He shakes with Andy and Issy then gestures to two chairs in front of the desk.

"Now, what can I do for you today?"

"Detective Ruiz and I are investigating the zombie murders, Dr. Birnbaum. You've heard of them, haven't you?"

Dr. Birnbaum offers them a half-smile. "Yes, yes, of course; it's all over the news." The smile widens. "You don't think one of our patients is involved, do you?"

"You tell us, Doctor," replies Molinaro. "Are any of your patients big young men in their early twenties who are schizophrenic and/or on strong psychotherapy drugs like Thorazine?"

Dr. Birnbaum folds his hands in front of him. "Well, we are certainly treating several schizophrenics and some split personality disorders, but only a few are men in their twenties. Most are older, and I assure you, Detective, they are harmless. Would you like to talk with one?"

Without waiting for an answer, Dr. Birnbaum motions for Nurse Carol, who has been waiting discreetly outside.

She pokes her head inside, smile at the ready. "Yes, Dr. Birnbaum?"

"Carol, can you do me a favor and bring David Wyche in?"

"Of course, Doctor," Carol replies then moves swiftly down the hall. A few minutes later, she returns with a pale, clean-shaven man of about twenty-five. The detectives take one look at David Wyche and are instantly reminded of a gentle giant. His six-foot, three-hundred-pound frame is sharply contrasted by the almost childish,

shaggy brown hair curled at the ends and a big toothy smile. He also has what Issy recognizes as an open bite dental occlusion, causing a slight drool and showing off a large tongue and puffy gums.

"Hi, David," Dr. Birnbaum says gently, "this is Detective Molinaro and his partner, Detective Ruiz."

"Hiya," responds David, but he is staring past the detectives.

As Andy continues to observe David's body language and overall demeanor, Isabella Ruiz quietly leaves the office and moves into the day room, where she finds a man orderly cleaning up a breakfast tray thrown to the floor by one of the patients.

"Hi there," she says, flashing her shield, "I'm Detective Ruiz. Can you spare a few moments..." She reads the name on his badge. "...Orson?"

Orson looks around. "Yes, ma'am, but just a few. I'm very busy."

"I can see that. Are you always this busy?"

"Yes, these people need twenty-four-seven looking after."

"Goodness, Orson, how do you keep track of them all?"

"We do our best, Detective."

Sensing an opening, Issy gives him a sympathetic nod. "I can't imagine...."

"Yeah, you wouldn't believe how many patients go missing."

"*Missing?*"

"Yes, ma'am. We find some of them wandering downstairs or outside on the grounds between here and the hospital."

"Really, do any go missing for a long time?"

"Yeah, some don't show up for three or four days." Orson snorts humorously. "Strange thing is, some come back here after the doctors discharge 'em. When they have to be here, they want to escape; when they leave, they decide they like it here better."

"Are any missing now?"

"I'm sure there are, but off the top of my head, I can't tell you who."

"Thanks for the information. Oh, by the way, do you know of any younger patients who have tattoos on their left arm?" Issy makes a circular motion on her own arm to demonstrate. "Just below the shoulder...?"

Orson thinks for a moment. "Yeah, one does for sure. Some sort of a flower and a heart, I think. There may be others too but—"

"Right. Not off the top of your head," Issy finishes his sentence as she scans the patient common areas. She looks into the TV room, the day room, the kitchen. All seem clean and orderly, and although most patients seem detached from reality, none seem violent. None have a tattoo.

Just then, the elevator door opens, and a nurse and an orderly emerge, chatting amiably as they head for the main desk. They do not see the glassy-eyed man half-limp/half-shuffle toward the elevator and slip inside. Issy debates for a beat, then rushes over to get in with him. The man looks at her for a long moment then presses the number-one plastic button. On the way down, she hears him mumbling, and although she cannot make out the words, she can tell he is repeating the same thing over and over again. When the elevator opens onto the ground floor, he shuffles right out the front door and walks aimlessly toward the parking lot. No one tries to stop him. No one knows.

Great security system, Birnbaum, Issy thinks as she heads back inside.

***

Four floors up, Detective Molinaro's questioning of David Wyche is much less informative.

"David," he asks, trying to imitate Birnbaum's soothing tone, "can I ask you some questions?"

"Why are the lights flashing?" David replies. "I don't like Dr. Birnbaum's room. The lights always bother me."

Molinaro, who has observed no flashing lights, shoots Birnbaum a perplexed look before turning back to David. "Do you or any of your friends here have a tattoo?"

"We watch television all the time. I really like 'The Ellen Show'. She's real funny."

Dr. Birnbaum chuckles softly. "He's disassociated, Detective. I'm afraid he won't be able to help you much."

"I see that," Andy says, trying to keep the frustration from his voice. "Doctor, do you happen to have any patients with Walking Corpse Syndrome?"

Dr. Birnbaum draws back in genuine surprise. "Wow, I'm impressed, Detective. Walking Corpse Syndrome is very rare." Then, without waiting for a response, he looks over at Carol. "One more favor, my dear. Can you find Mrs. Boykin for the detective?" He then turns to the young man. "David, why don't you go back to your friends in the TV room."

Carol escorts David Wyche out of the office and halfway to the TV room. Seeing his familiar place of entertainment, David breaks away from the nurse's light hold and, with a rapid shuffling gait, moves quickly toward it.

Five minutes later, Nurse Carol brings Mrs. Boykin into Birnbaum's office just as Detective Ruiz returns from her investigation. She and Andy share a brief look in which he conveys that he learned absolutely nothing. She nods almost imperceptibly, then they turn their attention Mrs. Boykin.

The thin, wiry woman in her mid-forties with light brown hair and a fair, freckly complexion bears no physical resemblance to the other "zombies," yet she bears the same despondent stare.

Though she barely acknowledges the two detectives, she does volunteer in an unemotional monotone, "My heart is dead. I can't feel it. My lungs are dead. I can't feel me breathe. My whole insides are dead. I am dead."

Detective Ruiz moves in front of Mrs. Boykin and takes her hand. "You're not dead, Ms. Boykin," she says softly. "We can see you, we can hear you, and I can even see you breathing."

For the briefest of seconds, Mrs. Boykin meets her eye. "You don't know. You don't know. No one knows. My body is dead." Then her gaze reverts to that same lifeless stare.

Seeing that the interview is over, the two detectives rise from their seats and thank Dr. Birnbaum and Nurse Carol for their time. Nurse Carol then escorts them back to the elevator, this time leaving them to ride alone so she can rejoin her charges. They exit the building and cross the parking lot with long, purposeful strides, each wanting to put as much space as possible between themselves and that depressing place.

"Well, that was a bust," Andy says as they reach the car. "We don't know any more now than we did before."

Issy stops, her hand on the door handle. "Well, Andy, that's not exactly true."

"Don't hold out on me, Ruiz." He slides into the driver's seat and waits for her to get in.

"Okay. Old Dr. Birnbaum might seem to be nice and cooperative, but the truth of the matter is he has no control of his patients. They're seriously understaffed to deal with such complex cases. According to the orderly I spoke with, many of the patients come and go; sometimes they're gone for days, and during that time, they're either off their meds or, even worse, overdosing on them."

She goes on to tell him about the man she followed into the parking lot.

"Sounds like you think Birnbaum was intentionally hiding something...."

"I *know* he was. Think about it, he chose the two patients you interviewed because he knew they wouldn't be any help. The question is, *why* is he hiding something? It could be as simple as he doesn't want us to know he's shitty at his job, but I don't think so. Call it a gut feeling or woman's intuition, but something's just not right."

Andy mentally reviews his conversations with Birnbaum and Carol and the observations of the patients. It all seemed legit at the time, especially since it seemed to align with what Merriweather had told them about such psychiatric disorders. However, he cannot not deny that Issy's theory makes sense.

"Okay, let's keep an eye on Birnbaum and his institute." Andy throws her a sideways smile. "Nice work, Ruiz. I think this partner thing may work out after all."

CHAPTER 9
Residency Revisted

In stark contrast to the dismal surroundings of the mental health institute, the Pain Management Institute run by Jacob B. Saltzman, MD, PhD is a monument not only to medicine but architecture as well. Occupying the entire first floor of the new Life Sciences Building, it has a lobby with stylish automatic electronic glass doors and brightly polished marble floors. The walls are tastefully decorated with murals and historical black and white pictures of the old hospital.

As lovely as it is, Robert Merriweather is much more impressed with the clinic itself. He read about the ten-thousand-square-foot space housing treatment beds, the latest monitoring devices, computer stations and a separate area for research, but as he walks through the reception area toward Dr. Saltzman's office this Thursday morning, he realizes the article had not done it justice. Dr. Saltzman's office is equally opulent, with a large mahogany desk and plush leather chairs; the walls are decorated with numerous plaques and awards celebrating his many accomplishments.

"The good Dr. Saltzman, I presume," he booms as he

sticks his head around the half-opened door and smiles at the short stocky man with a hooked nose and kind eyes. He's dressed in dark surgical scrubs with his name stitched over the shirt pocket.

"Bobby Merriweather!" he says, rising from his chair. "Glad you could make it. How long has it been, five years?"

"Something like that," replies Dr. Merriweather as he steps inside, "but you haven't aged a bit."

Indeed, aside from the male-pattern baldness that runs in his family, Saltzman, now in his mid-fifties, looks much the same as he did in residency.

The two shake hands and embrace with firm pats on the back for emphasis before sitting down in the plush leather chairs in front of the desk.

"Jake, I'm really impressed," Merriweather remarks as he gestures around, "and I don't mind admitting, a bit envious. How the heck did all this come about?"

"Research grants, industrial support, donors, you know, Bob. The fact of the matter is, control of chronic pain conditions without the use of opioids is a big industry and growing bigger every day. The recent press about the 'opioid epidemic' has helped. Our research here has made some big breakthroughs, and more are on the way, not dissimilar to your stem cell bone research." Saltzman's smile has just the slightest hint of wistfulness. "I guess we've both come a long way since our days as lowly first-year residents. Do you remember our first case together?"

Merriweather chuckles, remembering like it was yesterday his rotation on the anesthesia service. "Yes, and in particular your grand entrance into OR 8."

"Well, how was I to know that you guys made the dammed tile floor so slippery that with my first step I would fall on my ass, slide across the floor, and crash into the scrub nurse. What a sight that was—her straddled on top of me, all wide eyes and disheveled hair."

Both men burst out in howling laughter.

"As I recall," Merriweather gasps, "it all started with the drug pusher they brought up from the ER...."

The man still had on the long leather jacket he'd arrived at the hospital in. He also had a double-barreled, short-range shotgun blast to the abdomen and was gushing blood. The ER boys only had time to put the compression suit on his legs after placing a femoral line. When he got to the OR, Merriweather, who was on first call, quickly got an oral tube in him.

"Then along comes cowboy Bill Lester and his trauma team...."

"Right," Saltzman adds, "and Bill rips off the leather jacket, and out flies a bunch of broken bags of cocaine and cash.

Now red-faced with laughter, Dr. Merriweather recounts how the team looked on in amazement as white dust filled the air and twenty-dollar bills fluttered down to paper the floor.

"But the fun *really* started," Merriweather continues, "when Lester splashed about a gallon of Betadine antiseptic on the gushing wound. The mixture of cocaine, blood and Betadine created a floor as slippery as oil, which is what made your grand entrance possible." He pauses to wipe his eyes. "It was like an 'I Love Lucy' episode."

"...Or a mud wrestling match!" Saltzman adds. "All of us trying to pump blood into the guy while rolling on the floor and falling back every time we tried to get up." He lets out a sigh. "I wish we had cell phones back them. I would've taken a picture of you with your blood-soaked scrubs and cap covered with cash and white powder stuck on them like Christmas tree ornaments."

"Yeah what a mess that was...." Their laughter subsides as Merriweather recalls the farce's sobering conclusion. After fifty-two units of blood, Lester had called it a mortal wound and stopped trying to fix the aorta and inferior vena cava. "And unfortunately a futile effort from the very beginning."

They fall silent for a moment, neither quite able to believe all the years that have passed since that night. "Speaking of medical—and in this case, media—circuses, I'm assuming you've heard about the recent zombie murders...."

"Of course I have! The police are taking a lot of flak about it in the press." Saltzman shakes his head. "Media circus, indeed."

"Yes, and the two detectives taking the heat are friends of mine. I suggested to them that these zombies might be drug-crazed young men from the neighborhood. What drugs out there could cause such a state?"

"Too many, Bob," Saltzman says with another shake of his head, "There are the old standbys like crack, LSD, not to mention crystal meth and amphetamines, but I would also look into the new ones, particularly CAP and Basalt. Both are known to create the violent aggression similar to that of crystal meth and which has been attributed to these 'zombies'. You remember the attack on the homeless guy by what the press called the 'face eating attacker'? He was so out of his mind that the police had to kill him to get him off the victim. The ME's office concluded there was no Basalt in the attacker's body, but that's because they only examined the blood. If they had examined the brain or even the spinal fluid, believe me, they would've found it."

"Where does one get CAP and Basalt?"

Saltzman shrugs. "You can get it on the street if you know where to look. I'm sure the Narco unit can bring your detectives up to speed on that. In the meantime, I'll send you some articles on these drugs that will help you explain it to your detective friends."

"Thanks, Jake. Now, you mentioned on the phone that you needed my help as well. About what?"

"Are you and your sons still skin and scuba divers?"

Merriweather smiles at the mention of his boys and their shared passion for the sport. "Yeah, my boat's on a rack at Murray Marina in Key West, and we go every chance we get, though it's not nearly enough." The smile deepens. "Why, would you like a lesson?"

"No, nothing like that. I'm actually wondering if you could get me some lionfish. I understand they're all over our reefs now."

"Funny you should ask," Merriweather says, "I actually participated in one of the sponsored lionfish roundups."

Though native to the Indo-Pacific, lionfish have become, thanks to a rapid reproductive cycle and few natural predators, a significant presence in local waters. Some aquarium hobbyist probably released them into the wild, then nature took its course. The Florida Fish and Wildlife Commission recently declared open season on them and an unlimited harvest, just to reduce their numbers.

"The question is, why in the world do you want them?"

"I'm not planning on eating them, if that's what you're thinking." Saltzman waits for Merriweather to roll his eyes before continuing. "The poison in their spines that causes so much pain can also be used as a painkiller, just like the poison in the glands of puffer fish and the venoms of some snakes and scorpions. Heck, if I remember things right, you used curare as a muscle relaxant on the guy we were just talking about."

Merriweather nods in agreement. Throughout history, even deadly poisons such as digitalis, which stops the heart, and curare, which African tribes used to poison spears and arrows, have been turned into valuable medicines.

"Jake, you never cease to amaze me. We need to brainstorm more often, heck, we need to get together more often. I haven't laughed this hard since I don't know when."

Merriweather looks at his watch and sighs. "Now, I've gotta get going, and I'm sure you do too, but we'll talk more when I bring you the lionfish."

The two stand and once again go through the ritual of shaking hands and heartfelt embraces. Merriweather is nearly to the door when he turns back to his friend. "Oh, I nearly forgot. Can you accept one of my second-year residents for a rotation on your pain management service? He's sharp, he's passionate, and he's read all your papers. I think he'd be an asset."

"Consider it done. Just send him over, and we'll put him into the schedule. There's a lot he can learn here."

"Of that, Jake," Merriweather says, "I have no doubt."

Chapter 10
More Frustration

As Dr. Merriweather leaves the Life Sciences Building, happy to have reconnected with his friend, Issy Ruiz and Andy Molinaro are walking over to the Veterans Hospital, just west of the County Hospital and its adjoining mental health unit. As they cross 14th Avenue, Andy pulls his ringing cell phone from his suit pocket. Issy can tell from the way he answers that he's speaking to Chief Russell.

"That was the Chief," he confirms after ending the call. "She says the two murders at the diner were probably zombie murders too." He rolls his eyes. "Dammit, even I'm calling them zombie murders."

Issy smiles. "I caught myself doing it earlier. Maybe this trip to the VA will prove once and for all that there is a rational, human explanation for all this, like PTSD and meds with lousy side effects."

"One can only hope," Andy says wryly. "Literally, all we have is hope, because right now we've got nothing else to go on. Oh, and by the way, Chief said local news Channel 8 is going to give a daily update on the zombie murders starting today at five." He gives her a sideways glance. "Guess who they're interviewing."

Issy looks at him for a moment, then her eyes widen. "No! Don't tell me it's C.C. Murphy!"

"Okay, I won't tell you."

"Really, Andy? She's going to rake us over the coals!"

"Yup. We better get some good leads fast."

Fast, they soon learn, is a relative term. Despite showing their badges and identifying themselves as homicide detectives, Andy and Issy are required to remove all metal objects from their pockets and wait to go through security scanners with everyone else. The hospital is enormous, with fourteen floors and God knows how many employees, all of whom seem to be entering the building at the same time. Several minutes later, Andy and Issy finally reclaim their cell phones and pocket change and head down the main hall toward the staircase the security guard told them about.

"Glad we only have to go to the second floor," Andy mumbles as they climb the stairs.

Issy smiles and points to a sign directing them to Room 210-A. Once there, they again pull out their badges and show them to the receptionist. "We called earlier," Andy says after giving their names. "We're here to see Dr. George Bradley."

"Of course, Detectives. He's just finishing up a meeting with the Chief of Medicine. Have a seat, and I'll let him know you're here."

About ten minutes later, the door to Dr. Bradley's office opens. A tall, lanky man exits, and another man, presumably Dr. Bradley, is about to close the door without acknowledging the two detectives. Andy quickly gets up and places a gentle but firm hand on the handle.

"Dr. Bradley, I'm Detective Andy Molinaro and this is my partner, Detective Ruiz ... from Miami homicide...." He notes Bradley's rather cold stare. "We called earlier. We really need to talk to you."

"Detective," he replies flatly, "I have little time for such things, and let me remind you this is a federal facility." He shakes his head dismissively. "You have no jurisdiction here."

"Doctor, we don't want to interrogate you. We just want to ask you a few straightforward questions."

"Okay, but I only have a few minutes, and you can call me *Colonel* Bradley."

"Yessir," Andy says, trying hard not to be sarcastic.

As they enter his office, they indeed notice a block bearing the name George W. Bradley II Col US Marine Corp prominently displayed on the desk. In his early fifties, Colonel Bradley is almost as tall as Andy Molinaro and equally fit, with a firm muscular torso beneath his white clinic coat. He steps aside to let them enter, his eyes following Issy's shapely form as she walks over to one of his chairs and sits down. Finally, and seemingly with great effort, he turns his attention back to a very annoyed Andy.

"Colonel Bradley, we're investigating the recent murders in the area, and we wanted to discuss the possibility that returning veterans with post-traumatic stress disorder may be involved."

Immediately, the colonel's demeanor changes from aloof to indignant. "Now just wait a minute! You are talking about these ridiculous 'zombie' murders, aren't you? You people are on the hot seat, so you decide to come down here and point fingers at my vets!" He sees the uneasy look on Molinaro's face. "Our veterans risk their lives over there, and when they get home, they receive only the very best care. You civilians don't understand our military medicine. Come to think of it, you don't understand medicine at all." He snorts in disgust. "Look at the mess you've made of your so-called Affordable Care Act."

In the awkward silence that follows, Molinaro realizes that he indeed has misgivings about being here. It is much easier for him to believe that druggies are the culprit.

"Colonel," Issy says calmly, "you don't need to get upset. We're only seeking the truth. If a veteran with PTSD is involved, wouldn't you want to know about it so he can be helped and before he hurts someone else?" She leans forward, a sympathetic look on her face. "It's clear you only want the best for your patients, and we want the same."

Now it's Bradley's turn to fall silent, though from his expression, Molinaro's not sure whether he's considering Issy's point or her bra size.

"I can assure you, Detective Ruiz, that all of our veterans with PTSD are adequately treated and couldn't possibly participate in a murder. That said, HIPAA precludes me from sharing any of their medical information with you, as I'm sure you know. I also must inform you that I can only cooperate with federal investigations, so unless you and your partner are also with the FBI or CIA, this conversation must end here." He shuffles some papers on his desk. "Now if you'll excuse me, I have a lot of work to do."

Thoroughly annoyed by the man's arrogant and condescending attitude, not to mention the lecherous looks he's giving Ruiz, Andy dispenses with the politeness. "As a former FBI agent myself, I'm well aware of the limitations of this investigation. I also understand that if you wanted to help us, you could. You know, Colonel Bradley," he says rising from his chair, "I still have some friends in the Bureau. I wonder how you'd fare in an FBI investigation into how you really manage our returning veterans." Then, with a quick, hard nod of his head, Andy walks out of the office.

Still in the role of good cop, Issy says, "Good day, Colonel." As she follows her partner from the room, she can feel Bradley's appreciative eye on her rear.

Andy waits until they're off the grounds and out of earshot. "That was the last straw. First Birnbaum, now Bradley. Doesn't matter whether they're a doctor or a retired soldier, all these administrators want to do is cover their asses."

Issy waits for him to finish, then shrugs. "The man is a jerk."

Andy looks down at her for a beat then bursts out laughing. "That's one of the things I love about you, Issy," he says as he throws an arm around her shoulders, "your uncanny ability to sum up any situation in the most highly insightful and succinct way possible."

CHAPTER 11
Clues Emerge

A few hours later, the grim-faced detectives arrive at the squad. It's nearly noon, the time when they would normally be discussing where to go to lunch, but after dealing with the murder scene at the diner, neither Issy nor Andy can even think of eating. As they recount the gruesome details, they can see their disgust and frustration mirrored on Chief Russell's face.

"Well, you two better have some suspects, or at least a couple of real leads. I spent the entire morning on the phone with everyone from the mayor to our damned district congresswoman and a hundred other pains in the ass in between. I know I don't have to remind you of the bashing we took from eye witness news last night."

Andy and Issy nod in unison. C.C. Murphy had indeed done a hatchet job on the Miami PD with her comments about how the bumbling "glamour detectives" couldn't solve the case.

"I mean, how fast do you have to be," the loathsome woman quipped, "to keep up with *zombies*?"

Chief Russell leans forward, eyebrows raised. "Forgive me for saying this, but what a bitch."

"You can say that again," Issy mumbles while Andy nods in agreement.

"We do have leads," he says, "but it's complicated. I'll get to that part in a minute. The good news is we may have DNA profiles on two of the suspects. The lab boys analyzed the blood traces on the broken broomstick— two different sources, neither of them the victims'. We're running the sample through the national database now."

"Well, that's certainly more than we had this morning," Chief Russell replies. "Now why don't you tell me about the complicated part...?"

Issy takes over. "There are numerous psychiatric diseases and psychotherapy drugs that can create a zombie effect. There are also some street drugs that do the same. Dr. Merriweather is researching them for us. Andy and I went to the Miami Dade Hospital psyche unit and the VA Hospital but got little information." She glances at Andy. "We did learn something important, though; both units are stonewalling and quite possibly hiding something."

Andy breaks in. "I agree, Chief. Colonel Bradley, the Chief VA Administrator, is a spit and polish ex-marine and, if you'll forgive my language, a real ballbuster. He played the federal jurisdiction card, so, though I hate to ask, we're going to need help from the NCIS or FBI. Issy and I can handle Dr. Birnbaum's psyche unit ourselves and look into whatever Merriweather digs up."

Chief Russell slowly nods. "Nice work, detectives. You know I'd always rather someone ask for help than slow the process by trying to take on everything themselves.

And speaking of help, I'm sure the congresswoman will feel the sense of duty she so clearly articulated to me on the phone and get the feds to look into the Colonel's activities."

***

As Issy and Andy are meeting with Chief Russell, Dr. Merriweather is with his graduate fellow, Dr. James Glanville, and Chief Resident, Dr. David Montel. The three have finished the morning run of bone marrow samples using flow cytometry and are now looking over the results.

"James, David do you see a correlation here?"

Dr. Glanville spends nearly a minute looking over two Excel sheets of research data while Dr. Merriweather stands behind both of them with a knowing grin.

"Yes, yes, I can see!" Glanville says "The CD34+ cell correlates with the greatest amount of bone regeneration."

"That's it, James. The CD34+ bone marrow cell is the main signaling cell that turns on new bone formation. It's likely the cell that's producing our best jaw replacement results. We need to confirm this, but it could have far reaching importance for many bone-wasting diseases, from the simple bone loss around teeth to those that involve the entire skeleton, such as osteoporosis. You know, Arnold Caplan, the original bone stem cell discoverer, may just be right. He contends that the importance of stem cells is more to signal the workings of other cells than to reproduce itself. He has also suggested that the MSC designation of 'mesenchymal stem cells' be changed to 'medicinal signaling cells'."

The excitement of a small but significant research finding is interrupted by the rumbling of Glanville's stomach and the realization that it's five o'clock. They've been engrossed in their study and haven't eaten all day—and this day is far from over. In a little less than two hours, Steve Turner and Bevo St. Claire, the Haitian man whose tumor they will remove, will be landing at Miami Airport, and Merriweather, Glanville and Montel will be there to meet them.

They pull out the somewhat stale sandwiches they grabbed earlier from the research building's cafeteria—a meal that, for Dr. Merriweather, is made palatable by his favorite beverage and "the nectar of Waco Texas"—Dr. Pepper.

While eating, Dr. Merriweather reads over the articles about Basalt and CAP sent to him by Dr. Saltzman, while the two younger doctors peruse their cell phones for voice mail, text messages, and some nonmedical news. The three hardly say a word to each other for nearly fifteen minutes before Dr. Merriweather breaks the silence.

"Well, I'll be … it seems that all the street drugs exert their effect on the brain by interrupting sodium channels."

Glanville and Montel look up from their cell phones and say, almost in unison, "Is that important?"

"Well, think about it. One of the most common drugs

used by every dentist and oral and maxillofacial surgeon is the local anesthetic, such as xylocaine or novocaine. These work by discharging the electricity in the nerve; they open up calcium channels, rendering the nerve dormant. The patient feels numb, and you can then cut into tissues, remove a tooth, et cetera without causing pain. Well, what if part of the brain went dormant or numb, like a peripheral nerve?"

"Yes," Dr. Glanville replies, "but as you said, local anesthetics affect calcium channels. The drugs you mentioned a moment ago affect sodium channels."

"Correct, but what does opening the calcium channels do to the nerve electrically ready to conduct an impulse like pain?"

Glanville thinks for a beat. "Oh, I see. The open calcium channels allow the sodium into the nerve itself, and that's what discharges the nerve so it can't conduct electrical impulses."

"Exactly, James. A direct effect on sodium channels would be even more potent and long lasting, not to mention the many effects it would have on the brain." Merriweather smiles. "My old friend Jake Saltzman may have just given us the explanation for how these drugs are causing the zombie-like behavior." He glances at his watch. "I have just enough time to call Andy and Issy before we head to the airport."

✶✶✶

At six p.m. sharp, the three climb into Dr. Merriweather's minivan. "Remember," he says as he eases into rush hour traffic, "tonight we'll get Mr. St. Claire settled in the hospital. Tomorrow, you two will get his lab tests done and ready for the surgery Monday. I'll be in the office tomorrow, but on Saturday, I'll be spearfishing with my sons off Key West. Sunday, I'll return to talk to him about the details of his surgery, which reminds me, he only speaks Creole, so we'll need an interpreter."

Merriweather glances at the two young doctors. "Remember, this man has lived in the mountains of Haiti all his life and has no education or any real socialization. The hospital will seem like a strange world to him, and much of what transpires around him will be frightening, so he must be handled with the utmost caution and respect. Also, ensure his privacy as best as you can. Many, including other doctors and nurses, will want to see his huge tumor for curiosity's sake. I don't want to see any photos of him on the internet, okay?"

"Got it, Dr. Merriweather. Now what about the press?"

"After I talk to him and get his consent, I'll let one TV affiliate interview him, just like with any US citizen."

They spend the rest of the drive discussing St. Claire's upcoming surgery, excited by the prospect of ending this man's suffering and hopefully helping him live a more normal life.

***

At about the same time, in the heart of Coral Gables, four young men—two black, two white and all of them large—walk single file up to the night custodian's door at Saint Bellarmine High School. The one at the head of the line politely knocks and says, "Mr. Sherman, it's us. Are you in?"

Roger Sherman, a sixty-something black man of short stature, cleanly shaven and with short graying curly hair opens the door to see Reginald Doyo standing there.

"I'm always in for you boys," he says, smiling with grand-fatherly affection. "How you doing, Reggie?" Without waiting for an answer, Sherman tries to peer around him. "And Big Cat Thompson, is that you? You're so damned big, but I can hardly see you behind Reggie here."

"Hey, Mr. Sherman." Big Cat chuckles.

"Alright, and how about the other two—John, mhm, okay, but you're still blocking for my favorite QB. Come on out from behind him, Charles."

The other two boys call out their greetings, then Reginald Doyo, the obvious leader of the foursome, says, "Thanks, Mr. Sherman. We certainly do appreciate you letting us workout here all the time. I just hope we can repay the favor someday."

Roger Sherman dismisses the thanks with a shake of his head. "Boys, you've already paid me and this whole school back many times over with your two state championships and all." He gestures toward the dragon of St. Bellarmine along with the inscription "St. B/HS", tattooed on Reggie's left arm. "I remember when you guys got those tattoos for good luck right before your last state championship game."

Grinning, the other three boys rotate their left arms to display their matching ink.

"I just hope," Sherman adds, "that you guys get through your rehab and on to college football where you belong."

He then leads the foursome to their old high school gym with all its up-to-date exercise machines and dead weights. As the last—and at six-foot-three-inches and two-hundred twenty-five pounds, the smallest—passes Sherman, the custodian squeezes the young man's right arm. "Get that arm going again, boy. They didn't call you 'Chucking Charlie Harper' for nothing."

The young men laugh as they move to their favorite work-out machines. Sherman watches curiously as each pulls an oddly-shaped blue medical inhaler out of their gym bags and places it down next to them.

"Hey, why do you boys need inhalers? You got asthma or something?"

"No, it's nothing like that," replies John Malnicki, known in the area as "The Iron Wall" after a highly successful stint as Saint Bellarmine's offensive tackle. "It's just pain meds to help us get through rehab."

"Well, it better not be steroids, boys. You know all the colleges are testing for that now. Besides," Sherman says, smiling proudly, "you guys don't need steroids. You're too good the way you are."

With that, Sherman leaves them to their workout and begins his own, making his nightly rounds of the entire school, adjacent parking lot and outdoor stadium.

CHAPTER 12
Voodoo Magic

In the international concourse of Miami International Airport, just outside the Café Cubano coffee hut with its patrons sipping traditional coladas and *cortaditos*, the three doctors scan the steady stream of passengers disembarking the flight from Haiti. Drs. Glanville and Montel are particularly impatient as they await the appearance of their patient and his escort, in part due to the anticipation of being involved in such an unusual and challenging case, and partly because they're weary of the quizzing Dr. Merriweather has put them through for the past hour. Although they usually enjoy and seek out Dr. Merriweather's one-on-one style of teaching "real medicine," tonight, their minds are just not into it.

Finally, they see a thin man of about six feet with a large white towel wrapped around his head. Only his eyes and nose are visible, but there is no mistaking the overtly protruding lower jaw. He is flanked by a shorter man, just five feet seven inches, wearing a Toledo, Ohio Fire Department jacket. The three approach Steve Turner and Bevo St. Claire with outstretched hands and, after a brief welcoming, lead them toward the exit. The terminal is crowded with people waiting for friends, relatives and significant others, yet the towel-headed man draws only a few curious stares.

The five men are quiet until they reach the parking lot and Dr. Merriweather's waiting minivan, then Mr. Turner breaks the silence. "Doctors, I can't tell you how grateful I am and how much this means to Bevo. As I mentioned on the phone, he's considered an outcast in his community. They believe he has an evil spell on him and that some voodoo shaman is keeping him in this condition. He thinks you're a *good* voodoo shaman."

Dr. Merriweather laughs. "Mr. St. Claire is very astute. In a few hundred years, our successors will look back on us as primitive witch doctors who treated tumors by cutting out body parts, burning the hell out of them with radiation or poisoning them with chemotherapy."

"Maybe so," Turner replies, "but in the here and now, you're an answer to his prayers. You know, Bevo may be illiterate, but he's actually very smart. He's also sorry about the plight of his people and the problems they face back home. Given a chance, he could be a leader in his community."

"Mr. Turner, you told me this tumor, which we call an ameloblastoma, has been slowly growing for about sixteen years. Why does he want to have it removed now? Is it the difficulties it causes with eating and/or speech? Is it the weight of it?"

"Please, just call me Steve. I'm sure those are all contributing reasons, but he tells me that his goal is to get married and get a job."

"Wow, he's smart. I guess you understand and speak Creole then."

Steve shrugs. "Just enough to get by."

Traffic has lightened up, and just forty minutes later, the minivan pulls up to the back door of the hospital. As Dr. Merriweather parks his vehicle, the other three rush Bevo to a private suite on the third floor so as to avoid potential onlookers. Merriweather joins them a few minutes later with the ward's charge nurse. Together, they remove the towel to reveal a tumor the size of a basketball protruding as an expanded lower jaw. The charge nurse lets out a gasp of astonishment as Dr. Merriweather and his two residents quietly survey the tumor, which has greatly stretched the skin over the lower jaw and upper neck. Most alarming however are the lips, which over the past sixteen years have been stretched to a grotesque deformity reminiscent of African tribesmen who place increasingly larger and larger plates in their lips for ceremonial purposes.

Dr. Merriweather turns to his wide-eyed residents. "Notice the large blood vessels just under the skin. This tumor is larger than a newborn baby and has even more blood volume, which means our challenge during surgery will be to avoid excessive blood loss. Also notice the fluid leaking out of the part that's in his mouth. He has bitten into it with his upper teeth. Given the size of the tumor, the continual loss of this liquid has likely caused him to be protein deficient. Be sure to start him on protein supplements tonight."

As Dr. Merriweather reviews the orders with Glanville and Montel, the charge nurse and Mr. Turner introduce

Bevo to his new surroundings. After just a few minutes, the doctors hear a scuffle, followed by "NO! NO! NO! NO!" coming from the bathroom. The three rush in to observe Steve Turner and the charge nurse pulling Bevo's head out of the toilet.

"I'm sorry about this," Turner says. "Bevo thought the toilet was a spring to drink out of."

A mute chuckle erupts from the three doctors, but along with the humor comes the realization that Mr. St. Claire may not be able to cooperate with his post-surgery care and medications.

The temporary excitement over, Turner and the charge nurse go about showing Bevo his bed and things he has never seen before, such as a pillow and the light switch that turns daylight to darkness then back again with just the flick of a finger. Bevo St. Claire looks on with a combination of awe and trepidation at such "magic." Then the well-meaning charge nurse picks up the remote and turns on the television. Instantly, the room is filled with the sounds of Jerry Seinfeld arguing with George Costanza while canned laughter erupts in the background. Bevo takes one look at the images on the screen and lets out a loud, fearful cry. The others turn to see the man cringing in the corner of the room, gesturing with pawing hand motions and muttering something in Creole.

The horrified charge nurse quickly clicks off the TV while Mr. Turner rushes to Bevo's side. He tries to explain that the images are not black magic or voodoo as Bevo thought but a tool used by the good shaman, Dr. Merriweather, to get rid of the tumor. Using a soothing tone, he eventually manages to get Bevo to settle down and accept the "magic box."

"I think Mr. St. Claire has had enough of an introduction to modern technology," Merriweather announces calmly. "He's experienced sensory overload that I can actually relate to." His mouth splits into a grin. "I personally think the electronic medical record is an evil curse placed on us by a group of evil shamans we call politicians."

Glanville and Montel chuckle for they are well-aware of Merriweather's feelings on the subject.

"Mr. Turner," Merriweather continues, "you stay with Bevo tonight. My residents and fellows will do the medical workup tomorrow, and I'll be back to visit with both of you Sunday afternoon."

CHAPTER 13
The Impasse

It is nearly nine p.m. when Dr. Merriweather climbs back into his minivan and heads home. As he navigates the crowded Miami streets, he is still thinking about Bevo St. Claire, specifically his reaction to the television. It is amazing that in a world so completely reliant on technology, where people yearn to go "off the grid," there are still places where people don't even know a grid exists.

When he walks in the door, he is immediately greeted by the wagging tails of his three Labrador retrievers, Rocky, Tubby, and Libby. He squats down to return the hello and is rewarded by a few licks on the face.

"Well, at least your dogs still matter to you."

Startled, Dr. Merriweather straightens up to see Heather Bellaire, his girlfriend of several years, standing a few feet away. For a moment, he stands there, taking in the set of her jaw and steely gaze, and then it hits him—he and Heather planned to be together for an extended Friday to Sunday weekend.

"Oh no, Heather, I completely forgot! I'm so sorry."

"*Sorry?* You cancel on me three weekends in a row then

'forget' to get me at the airport, and all you can say is sorry? You know, Robert, I have responsibilities as well, and it's not always easy for me to drop everything and fly down here."

Robert eases out of his white lab coat and hangs it up in the hallway closet. Indeed, there are many demands on Heather's time; she's constantly juggling her responsibilities as a single mother of two sons with her position as Director of Acquisitions at El Cid Publishing in New York. Yet, no matter what else is going on in her life, Heather has always managed to make time for Robert, and although he has tried to do the same for her, it seems that over the past few months he has become increasingly absorbed in his own work. It is Heather's next statement, however, that lets him know the seriousness of his predicament.

"Well," she says, attempting a smile, "I guess I can forgive you for not picking me up at the airport since we'll have a weekend together, at long last."

Suddenly, the usually authoritative and in control surgeon is transformed into a stammering, apologetic boyfriend. "Uh, Heather, I..." he begins, then, unable to find the right words, he launches into a summary of recent events. "We have a case—a charity case—with an eight-pound tumor. I also have some significant additions to our research activities. Plus I had to cover the trauma team this week, which just so happened to have two major surgeries—one, a twenty-eight-year-old female shot in the cheek, the other a facial beating so nasty an eye had to be removed. In addition to that, Issy and Andy needed my help with a difficult murder case and—"

"Let me guess," Heather interrupts, "the zombie murder case?"

"You heard about that?"

"Yes, Robert, we have news in New York too," she snaps. "And if you had listened to any of my voicemails over the last few days, you'd know that I heard about it." She folds her arms across her chest. "What are you really saying, Robert?"

He sighs heavily. "I'm saying that I didn't just forget to pick you up at the airport, I forgot about *the weekend*. In fact, I promised Robbie and Ryan they could join me in a lionfish spearing session tomorrow. We're going to supply poison spines for Jake Saltzman's pain research and—"

Heather cuts him off again, this time with a tone he's never heard from her before. "Lionfish? Well, this certainly lets me know where I stand with you ... last in line, after your sons and your colleagues." She shakes her head. "You're never going to change. You're always going to be involved in this and that and then the other thing."

For the first time since he was a naïve teenager, he finds himself standing in front of a girl at a loss for words. "Heather, I—"

"Don't, Robert. I can now see why Veronica left you. She got more love and attention from her rescue animals than from you."

He pulls back as if slapped, and the fact that Heather is right makes the words no less painful. He knows his immersion in his profession and his research cost him his marriage to Veronica; it also created distance between him and his sons. Yet at the same time, he can't help but feel she's being unnecessarily cruel. Heather knows how hard he's been trying to close that gap, in part through bonding events like the one he planned for this weekend. Now mature young men in their mid to late twenties, Robbie, Randy, and Ryan understand the complexities of relationships. They have also accepted Heather and see her as the road to their dad's happiness. She, however, seems to be saying his boys are a roadblock. His only option is to be perfectly candid.

"Heather, I thought our relationship was going somewhere too. I can only say I screwed up, and you know how difficult that is for me to say. Maybe I'm not the right man for you, but I do love you. This is another difficult thing for me to say, but I do mean it."

Heather shakes her head sadly. "I believe you believe that, Robert, but I don't know. I'll just have to think this over. I'll stay in the guest room tonight and return to New York tomorrow. Heaven knows I have plenty of my own work to do. You do what you have to do with your sons and your doctor buddies, and we'll see how we feel about our relationship in the coming weeks."

Dr. Merriweather looks at her, knowing that for the moment there is nothing left to say. He nods in agreement and retires alone to his bedroom, one he has shared with Heather many times before.

He awakes the next morning to find that her anger has been replaced by an icy silence. Heather relents enough to let Robert drive her to the airport, but the trip is tense and void of conversation. It is only when he hands over her overnight bag that they look into each other's eyes. Heather offers him a small, despondent smile, and Robert places a light kiss on her forehead, then she disappears through the automatic glass doors.

CHAPTER 14
Killing at the Kegger

Dr. Merriweather spends the rest of Friday morning and early afternoon rounding on his other patients and seeing to it that Bevo St. Claire has had all the necessary blood tests and CT scans. Though outwardly he operates with the calm, rigorous efficiency he is known for, Heather's words and the uncertain future of their relationship weigh heavily on his mind.

By six p.m., Dr. Merriweather has hooked up with Ryan and Robbie, and they are heading down to the Keys for their spearfishing event. All experienced divers and spear fisherman, they are looking forward to the challenge of the hunt and an outdoors break from their intense schedules.

At around the same time, the four former high school athletes finish their daily workout at Saint Bellarmine and head north toward the University of Miami campus. After an intense regimen and several puffs of their inhalers, they are invigorated but have assumed the staring, non-blinking gaze and purposeful straightforward walk of a drug-induced zombie effect.

Thirty minutes later, they arrive at the lawn of the

Lambda Alpha Beta, or "LAB" as its originating members affectionately called it. Founded just five years ago, LAB is in its infancy compared to other Greek fraternities, some of which have been around for more than half a century. It is also notably less raucous as most of its members are geeks. Nevertheless, just before sundown, a keg party is about to begin as a prelude to tomorrow's football game against archrival Florida State. Although fraternity row is somewhat desolate at this time, the drum beat and din of music can already be heard emanating from several fraternity houses in the distance, letting the rest of the campus know the pregame parties are just a few hours away.

As they come upon it, the four athletes stare at the frat house with a flag bearing the big Greek letters Lambda-Alpha-Beta hanging over the porch. They hear the steady beat of hip-hop coming from inside the house and see two large beer kegs on the lawn guarded by a lone fraternity member.

"Hey, guys," he says with a friendly smile and curt wave, "you're a little early. Party's not for a few hours."

The foursome stares back at him, but they say nothing.

"Okaaay," he replies, already sorry he volunteered for this job. He then leaves his station to report the uninvited guests to fraternity president, Lawrence "Buzz" Guroff.

"Hey, Buzz," he says, leaning his body in the front door of the house, "we haven't even started yet and already we got party crashers."

Buzz emerges from the kitchen, a beer in hand. His lanky frame is dressed in khaki shorts, a plaid button-down shirt untucked and hanging over his belt, and sneakers.

"It's not those Lamb Chop guys from down the street, is it?"

"Heck no. These dudes are *big*. Lambda Chi Alpha doesn't have guys this big."

"Okay, I'll take care of it," Buzz says as he slips out the door and onto the porch.

Buzz Guroff is not only the president of Lambda Alpha Beta but of the university Student Council as well. As a political science major and campus organizer, he feels duty-bound to immediately resolve the situation.

"Excuse me, guys, but this is a private pregame...." He calls out, but his voice trails off as he recognizes them.

"Oh my God!" he exclaims to the beer keg guardian beside him. "It's the four horsemen from St. Bellarmine!"

"The four who of what?"

"Hell, they're legendary! Just last year, they won their second straight 6A football title by annihilating the so-called best team in the state, seventy-seven to seven. Reggie Dojo over there was the best defensive end ever, forty-two sacks in one year. The big guy is 'Big Cat' John Thompson. You remember the likes of the famous University of Miami defensive tackles, Russell Maryland, Warren Sapp and Vince Wilfork? Well, he would've been just like them. The small guy is Chucking Charlie Harper, the Rivals-dot-com number-one quarterback. And next to him is bad ass John Malnicki. He became known as The Iron Wall because no defender could get by him. He protected Harper so that he was never sacked, not even once, WOW!"

"How do you know so much about these guys?"

"I was three years ahead of them at St. Bellarmine and followed their 'careers,' so to speak. They were recruits of the U, but they all got hurt in their last championship game and are sitting out college this year. Too bad; we could really use these guys now."

Buzz steps down from the porch and approaches the four, unaware that his girlfriend Amy Hooten has followed him outside. She stands by the doorway, watching the exchange. "Are you guys here for the game tomorrow? Boy, if you were playing for the U, we would crush those FSU dirtbags. Come on and join us. The party will get started soon."

Buzz walks over to the keg so excited to be hosting the football stars that he doesn't notice their continued silence or their disassociated stares. He quickly pours a cup of beer and offers it to Charlie Harper only to be met with a powerful hand that sends the drink flying. Before he realizes it, big John Malnicki lifts him like a rag doll and throws him toward Big Cat Thompson. Huge arms tighten around Buzz like a vise, literally squeezing the life out of him. A few feet away, Reggie Dojo grabs the other young man and brutally smashes his head into the very beer keg he has been guarding. Then, as if on cue, the football stars drop their victims and calmly walk away from the yard.

The whole horrible incident has taken less than two minutes.

Amy Hooten, who has watched in horror from the porch, is frozen in shock and too terrified to scream. Slowly, she backs into house, mumbling, "Oh my God, oh my God," then goes to the phone to call campus police. Through the young woman's sobs, they hear the word "zombie" and immediately call for a campus-wide lockdown. They also call the Miami Homicide Bureau and ask for the detectives working the now-infamous murders.

Thirty minutes later, Detectives Molinaro and Ruiz arrive at yet another gruesome scene with two more bodies mutilated almost beyond recognition. The only description of the assailants comes from a lone, hysterical witness but matches those of the previous crimes. There is no obvious forensic evidence, and a thorough search of the campus yields nothing. Seven zombie murders in just one week, and once again the culprits are nowhere to be found.

CHAPTER 15
Even Zombies Get Homesick

John Malnicki and Big Cat Thompson hear the long-awaited footsteps coming up the narrow stairwell, then the sounds of keys jingling. The apartment door opens, and Reginald Doyo and Charlie Harper walk in, each carrying several brown paper bags. Within seconds, the heavenly aroma of Burger King Double Whoppers with cheese, fries, and onion rings permeates the room. It is a vast improvement over the usual musty smell of the small two-bedroom apartment where four men in their early twenties, not well versed in housekeeping, have been living for the past six months.

Malnicki and Big Cat eagerly take some of the overload from the arms of their two roommates and begin to parcel out who got what. Once it has all been sorted, the feeding frenzy begins, with Malnicki and Big Cat each wolfing down big bites of burger and fries and getting half of the mayonnaise and ketchup on their faces. In contrast, Reggie and Charles separate out their meal in distinct parcels and eat in a somewhat more refined manner.

"Hey, John, are you eating your burger or wearing it?" Charlie asks, his lips twisting into a smirk. "That shade of mustard goes well with your blonde hair."

Had anyone other than his teammate made such a joke, the aggressive right tackle would have responded with a smack, or at least a threatening look. Instead, he bursts out laughing, spraying Dr. Pepper out of his nose and half-chewed French fries from his mouth. The scene sets off boisterous laughter and finger-pointing reminiscent of "Animal House." Reggie says as much, for though the 1978 cult classic is ancient by their standards, it is still much beloved.

The hilarious mood continues for another half hour, with Reginald Doyo recalling the time Big Cat Thompson, then a lowly freshman, put his supporter cup on backwards, making it appear he had "crapped in his pants." Big Cat retorts by pointing out how just last year Reggie picked up a loose fumble and ran the wrong way. He got tackled in the end zone to score a safety for the opposing team. Their coach gave him the game ball with a compass taped to it, and for the rest of the season, Reggie was haunted by teammates' chants of "Which way Doyo—he don't know."

The laughter fades with their hunger, and silence replaces the noise echoing off the unadorned walls of the kitchen-slash-dining room area where they do most of their living.

Big Cat, his head now bowed, asks in a somber tone, "Reggie, when can we go home? My mama thinks I'm already at the U getting ready for spring practice. I don't like lying to her, and besides, what if she decides to visit?"

"It won't be much longer," Reginald Doyo replies as he licks the salt from the fries off his fingers. "Dr. Saltzman said he's ready for the final session that will cure our pain for good, without even using our inhalers."

John Malnicki joins in. "Yeah, man. We need to stick with the program. You're not wimping out on us, are you?"

"No, no, I'm with you guys, but we should be in class, not studying in here all day and working out only at night so no one recognizes us." He pauses to give his comrades a pointed look. "You have to admit it's weird."

"Sure it's weird," Charlie Harper concedes, "but it's better than being red-shirted and waiting to be made starters all over again. This way, the coach or trainer don't know about our injuries. They'll think we're just as good as we were last year—even better through our workouts—and keeping up with our academic requirements."

Big Cat shakes his head. "I get it, but how come after working out we always end up back here and don't even remember how we got home?"

In response, John Malnicki tosses Big Cat one of the controllers to their Xbox and turns it on. "Come on, let's stop whining. I'll beat your butt in either Dungeons and Dragons or Assassin's Creed. Your choice."

Once again the mood changes, at least for Big Cat and John Malnicki, who are sitting together on the old musty and stained sofa completely absorbed in their video contest. As they push the four buttons with intensity and speed, Reginald Doyo and Charlie Harper remain at the small kitchen table and engage in a more serious discussion.

"Reggie, you talk to Saltzman more than anyone. Is he really on the up and up?"

Reggie nods. "Sure he is. Saltzman is giving us his latest

pain killers—the ones no one else has. I mean, look how the inhalers take the pain away so fast. So what if it only lasts a few hours and makes us sleep a while? It's still kinda experimental, which is why we need to keep it a secret for now. Anyway, we only got one more treatment to go. Dr. Saltzman told me it'll be in his pain center and last for a couple days, but then we're done. We'll be at the U in January, practicing by spring and playing next September. That was our plan, remember? We're on schedule."

"You're right. We've come this far, and we can't go back now. But, Reggie, this better work. Our money is getting low, and our parents will find out sooner or later." Charlie shakes his head. "I don't know how to even begin explaining all of this to them."

"I don't know either, but I trust Dr. Saltzman. Once we get our football scholarships, attend classes again, and play on the team, they'll understand."

CHAPTER 16
Lionfish

Saturday finds Drs. Glanville and Montel dutifully preparing Bevo St Claire for removal of the tumor and a bone graft to replace more than three quarters of his jaw. Mr. Turner and Marle Celestine, a native Haitian Creole interpreter, have done an excellent job in making Bevo understand the basics of the procedure; no one, however, knows how to explain that his jaw will be replaced by his own stem cells combined with recombinant human bone morphogenetic protein known as rhBMP, and that this stem cell's utilization is the end product of Dr. Merriweather's research. The notion of growing new bone rather than transplanting it from some other part of his body would seem like too much voodoo for Bevo, so they just leave it be.

While Bevo is undergoing his pre-surgical workup, Dr. Merriweather, Robbie and Ryan are aboard the *Fish R Nervous*, their twenty-seven-foot twin-hulled Sea Cat. Cruising along at thirty-five knots, the fishing boat heads toward the Tango wreck forty-five miles out on the Gulf side of Key West. By the time they reach the halfway point, Merriweather's sons are already preparing two very different sets of spear guns for their adventure. One set is the standard Riffe 42 banded spear gun used in most spear fishing tournaments. These spear guns are designed for large game fish such as big snapper, grouper and cobia. The other type of spear gun is especially designed for their target of the day, lionfish, and is the most efficient way to keep their father's promise to Dr. Saltzman. With more lance than gun, these consist of a straight aluminum shaft with three unbarbed but sharp tips. Fixed to the base is a large loop of a one-inch-round rubber band. The diver holds the lance at mid-shaft together with the stretched band. As the diver releases his grip, the lance juts out to impale any fish within four feet. It is perfect for lionfish, which are both slow-moving and potentially dangerous. The lack of barbs allows the diver to slide the impaled fish off without the risk of coming into contact with its poisonous spines.

As the *Fish R Nervous* skims over the calm sea, Merriweather admires the vast, beautiful landscape of blue-green water blending into an even bluer sky. The breeze created by the boat speeding along blows in his face. Normally, his everyday stress and demands would be a long way off, but he continues to be haunted by Heather's words.

Forty minutes later, they are anchored over the Tango wreck, a crumpled piece of metal left over from an old shrimp boat that went down over twenty years ago.

"Okay boys, let's sink the holding cage with the buoy marker on it. Remember, we are here to spear lionfish, not snapper or grouper. You can bring a Riffe gun down, but only shoot one fish and only if you get a good shot at it. Don't waste your airtime chasing a big black grouper around. It's eighty feet here, and we'll only have about twenty-five minutes of bottom time on compressed air. Don't forget to decompress as your decompression meter indicates."

"Got it, Dad," his sons say almost in unison. Though somewhat disappointed in limiting their spearfishing to lionfish, they are looking forward to depleting the population of what the Florida Marine Association labels as an invasive species dangerous to the natural marine life of the area. Even better, they're helping their father fulfill his promise to Dr. Saltzman in furtherance of his groundbreaking research.

With the boat securely anchored and a "Divers Down" flag mounted on the boat's T-top, they check out their gear just as an airline pilot would check his instruments before takeoff.

Finally, it's time to dive. Fully geared up in eighty-cubic-foot aluminum scuba tanks, regulators, and two spear guns in hand, the three men fall off the boat gunnels backwards into the Gulf waters. Even at eighty-four degrees, the water feels cool at first, but they quickly adjust and together begin to descend using the rope tied to the holding cage. About halfway down, they spot the tangled heap of metal with some shrimp boat netting still draped over it. The usual school of three-to-eight-pound mangrove snappers hovers over the wreck, swimming gracefully in and out of its holes and crevices. Amidst them are numerous smaller lionfish, beautifully adorned with their poisonous brown and purple spines spread out like the feathers of a peacock. As Dr. Merriweather checks out the anchor setting, his two sons go about impaling as many lionfish as they can. Their father joins them a few moments later, and soon the threesome are sliding impaled lionfish off their barbless three-pronged spears and into the holding cage. It seems they are only down there a few minutes when Dr. Merriweather's air gauge indicates only 500 psi of remaining air in his tank. He jerks his thumb upward, signaling to his sons that it's time to surface. As he and Ryan are about to ascend, they hear the spring of Robbie's Riffe spear gun go off. They turn in the direction of the sound in time to see Robbie coming around the Tango wreck. He has speared a big black grouper—the best eating and hardest-to-spear fish in Florida—in the twenty-pound class. The threesome spend five minutes at twenty feet just breathing while holding on to the anchor rope, and another ten minutes at ten feet to decompress the remaining nitrogen bubbles out of their tissues as indicated by the decompression meters attached to their regulators.

Once back on the boat, they compare notes and change scuba tanks for a second round. However, they plan an hour surface interval in order to remove more nitrogen from their systems and thereby reduce their decompression time on the second dive.

The second dive goes just as smoothly as the first with all three fully committed to their two-pronged mission: ridding the ocean off Key West of an invasive species and supplying Dr. Saltzman with hundreds of poisonous fish spines for his research.

It is with a sense of accomplishment that they return to

the dock at Murray Marina in Stock Island, adjacent to Key West Proper. The *Fish R Nervous* is met by Danny, a sixteen-year-old dockhand and boat cleaner.

As Danny ties the dock ropes to the port cleats of the boat, he asks, "Need your boat cleaned today, Doc? For an extra five, I'll even help you get your gear out."

"Danny, I'll give you an extra ten if you get all these tanks and other gear on the dock for us to wash off."

Dr. Merriweather hands Danny a twenty-dollar bill for the boat cleaning, plus the extra ten he promised. "Here's your money, but let us handle the cage. It has over sixty lionfish in it."

As Merriweather goes to refuel the boat, Robbie begins cleaning his grouper while Ryan dons the special metal-meshed gloves needed to handle the lionfish and the heavy scissors needed to cut off their spines. Danny starts unloading the scuba tanks and gear.

After just a few minutes, they hear Danny screech, "Dammit!" followed by "Ouch, ouch, ouch. WOW! That stings like shit!"

Dr. Merriweather looks over to see that Danny, in the course of moving the scuba tanks off their racks, somehow knocked over the holding cage and spilled several lionfish on top of his bare feet. To make matters worse, he's trying to remove the dead lionfish with his bare hands, which only leads to more stings.

Immediately, Merriweather and his sons rush over to him. As Ryan uses his gloves to remove the lionfish from around Danny's feet, Robbie and Dr. Merriweather get the boy out of the boat and onto the dock. Robbie then grabs his own pair of metal mesh gloves and helps his brother retrieve the fish.

Merriweather notes the multiple stings on the insteps of Danny's feet and several more on his hands. Then, looking him straight in the eyes, he asks, "Danny, are you alright? How do you feel?"

"I'm okay, Doc. My feet still sting, and they also feel kind of numb."

Keeping a watchful eye on Danny, Dr. Merriweather immediately grabs his cell phone and calls 911.

"Please don't call no ambulance, Doc," Danny implores him. "I'll be alright."

Ignoring him, Merriweather quickly tells the 911 operator the nature of their emergency as well as their precise location. Though Danny continues to insist he's feeling fine, Dr. Merriweather watches for the slow but certain onset of symptoms of lionfish venom. Sure enough, five minutes later, Danny starts screaming in pain.

Dr. Merriweather lays him down on the dock and tries to comfort him, but the boy's screams only grow louder, drawing a small crowd of fishing guides and their clients. Robbie and Ryan place the last lionfish back in the holding cage and bring over the first aid kit.

Merriweather shakes his head. "I'm afraid a first aid kit won't do any good in this instance. There is no reversing lionfish toxin. And because it's heat stable, hot water, which is used to decrease the pain of stingray toxin, won't work here. We just have to get him to the hospital for supportive care and hope his youth and general health will help him."

When he looks back down, he sees Danny has gone unconscious.

"Is he in shock, Dad?"

"I think so, Robbie. His pulse is slow, but he's actually breathing normally, although that's a bit slow too."

Just then, Fire Rescue arrives and immediately puts an oxygen mass on Danny. As Dr. Merriweather repeats the details for them, he notices the Fire Rescue machines registering a lower than normal but not dangerous blood pressure and pulse rate. Certainly, Danny is not in complete shock, at least not yet. Merriweather watches as Fire Rescue loads the still unconscious young man into their truck, then he hops in.

"Clean the boat and cut off the lionfish spines," he tells his sons, "then meet me at the hospital."

Later that evening, Dr. Merriweather consoles Danny's parents, giving them as much hope as he can without giving false hope. It is a puzzling case to be sure. Danny is in the intensive care unit but without the need for the basic support of his vital heart and lung functions. He's also, thankfully, not screaming in pain as he was earlier. On the other hand, he is lying there in a coma, and no one seems to know why.

CHAPTER 17
The Operation

By mid-afternoon on Sunday, Dr. Merriweather is back at his own hospital completing the presurgical preparation for Bevo St. Claire. Turns out he'd been right about Bevo's low blood protein levels, so he sees to it that Dr. Glanville has added albumin to his IV fluids and protein powder to his nutritional supplements.

Still, Danny is never far from his thoughts, and whenever he gets a chance, Merriweather calls the ICU in Key West to check on him. The news is always the same: Danny remains in a coma.

***

Early Monday morning, Dr. Merriweather and his team wheel Bevo into operating room number eight. He has already been sedated by the anesthesia team headed by Dr. Carlos Morales, as one of the doctors has to hold the tumor upright to prevent it from falling off to one side and dangerously twisting Bevo's neck.

A few miles away, Dr. Saltzman is elated to receive the

cooler full of lionfish spines Dr. Merriweather couriered to him. Atop the cooler is an envelope containing a note of caution about handling the spines and a short description of Danny's ordeal and condition. Saltzman makes a mental note to call and thank his friend, then he prepares to head to his lab.

Back at South Dade Hospital, Dr. Morales, at Merriweather's request, proceeds with a fiber optic scope intubation. Guided by the lighted fiber optic scope, he passes a breathing tube through Bevo St. Claire's nose, past the tumor bulge in the throat and through the vocal cords. Through this tube, Morales administers the anesthetic gases that will keep Bevo unconscious and free of pain for what is anticipated to be a twelve-hour surgery.

After the usual antiseptic preparation and draping of the skin of the neck and around the mouth, as well as the skin adjacent to the tumor, Dr. Merriweather and his team begin. As they make their initial incision in the neck from below the left ear clear around to the same area below the right ear, they are met with the numerous blood vessels they identified in their initial examination. As surgical team leader, Dr. Merriweather isolates each blood vessel, then each of the two residents places a vascular clamp on one end of the vessel. Dr. Merriweather transects the blood vessel between the two clamps, and each resident proceeds to tie the blood vessel shut below the clamp before it is taken off. This maneuver is repeated over and over again until the thinned-out skin and other tissues are peeled off the entire circumference of the tumor. After more than six hours of this intricate surgery, the tumor is isolated from the surrounding normal tissues with almost no loss of blood. Then, since the tumor is seen to arise from the chin portion of the lower jaw and extends back into the wisdom tooth area and forward as a jutting basketball-sized protuberance, it is sawed off below the joint area of the lower jaw on each side in an amputation fashion using a back and forth compressed air driven saw. Here, a momentary blood loss is soon controlled by the quick actions of the surgical team, who clamps the transected blood vessels from the bone on each side.

Once the tumor is separated from the back part of the lower jaw, it falls off under its considerable weight. Dr. Glanville actually has to brace himself while cradling the huge tumor as it falls away from the uninvolved portion of the lower jaw. He takes it to the scale used to weigh newborns and announces its weight as eight and a half pounds.

Dr. Glanville's sense of relief and accomplishment soon gives way to the realization that there is much more surgery to perform. Namely, the surgeons still must reduce the size and reshape the overstretched lower lip and then remove the stem cells from Bevo's hip bone via thin aspiration catheters for the planned bone graft.

After another six hours, both tasks are accomplished, and the lengthy incisions are closed. Bevo's breathing tube is removed and replaced with a tracheostomy tube through an opening in the windpipe. He is then taken to the recovery room with all involved noting Bevo's remarkably different appearance. He not only looks normal but is actually quite handsome. Beneath their smiles, however, the surgical team's optimism is tempered with caution as each knows that it can all fall apart from an infection or other complication. For now, the tired trio of surgeons will only celebrate it as a "so far so good" status, all the while knowing the surgery has created an astounding transformation.

***

While Dr. Merriweather and his team are in the last phase of the twelve-hour surgery, Colonel Charles Bradley parks his metallic blue jaguar in the parking lot of the Life Sciences Building, just a few blocks west of his own workplace at the Miami Veterans Administration Hospital. Bradley enters the building and, as he has done numerous times before, passes the receptionist and proceeds directly to the office of Dr. Jake Saltzman. When the doctor looks up from the article he is reading, Bradley cuts right to the chase.

"Okay, Dr. Saltzman, I got your message. Whatever your news is, it better be good. Our benefactors are getting antsy. Can I tell them that you're at least making progress?"

"Indeed you can, Colonel. Just this morning, my old friend Bob Merriweather sent the final ingredients for my formula, and I've spent the last several hours purifying and concentrating it. Final testing will begin today, and in less than three months, we'll have the proof you need."

"Why three months?"

"Come on, Charles, you know from your experience as a combat surgeon and your involvement with injured veterans that the main problems in pain control is addiction and that the wearing off of the pain medication requires re-dosing, usually at a higher dose. I've already resolved four subjects' pain for up to forty-eight hours but need to increase it further. The lionfish toxin Merriweather sent will add to and potentiate the effects of the puffer fish toxin and ciguatera toxin I'm currently using. It will now last much longer. It's the controlling substance I need."

If Saltzman is expecting congratulations, he's about to be disappointed.

"You're not going back on our agreement, are you?" Bradley says with narrowed eyes. "Because what you're describing is great, but it's not what our sponsors are supporting. My ten-million-dollar project leader fee and your Nobel Prize in Medicine is not going to be about a long-lasting pain killer … It *better* be about—"

Saltzman cuts him off. "Hold on there, Colonel. I know full well what our real goal is, and, the Heavens willing, you'll get your riches and I'll finally get my due recognition as the discoverer of the greatest medical find of the twenty-first century. However, do you think I would ever get an Institutional Review Board to approve a study using three deadly fish poisons for anything other than the noble goal of a cure-all for pain?" Saltzman does not wait for a response. "You know as well as I do that all research studies have to be registered. This one is registered with the NIH as a pain control study, which means that while I only get a pittance of research dollars, everything is legit and above board. No one will know our real goals until I have definite proof and our sponsors and I patent the formula."

Colonel Bradley smiles, dispelling some of the tension. "You are indeed clever, Saltzman. That's why we make such a good team."

Just then, the receptionist calls to tell Dr. Saltzman that four young men are here to see him. He looks at Bradley.

"So would you like to meet the test subjects?"

"Sure. Why not?" he replies, managing to convey that he really has no interest in Dr. Saltzman's subjects, just the outcome.

As Reginald Dojo, Big Cat Thompson, John Malnicki and Charles Harper enter the room, each carrying an overnight duffle bag, Colonel Bradley is taken by their physical size and muscular builds. Oh, the great things he could have accomplished with specimens like these in his old marine unit.

Before Colonel Bradley can offer more than a curt nod, Dr. Saltzman booms, "So, boys, are you ready for the big test? You'll be here for a couple of days, you know."

As usual, Reginald Dojo takes the lead. "We're ready, Doc. That's why we brought our bags."

"So I see. Hope you brought your inhalers as well. I'll need to put your new pain medication in them."

"We did, Doc." Reggie glances at the others. "But me and the guys are worried. Every time we take the medicine, it takes away all our pain and lets us sleep, but when we wake up we can't remember anything. It's like we were drunk or something."

Saltzman gives him an understanding nod. "The new pain medicine should stop that. Now if you go into the next room," he says, gesturing to the right, "my nurse will get you all set up with monitors to register your blood pressure, pulse, brain wave activity and other things. You'll be sleeping like a baby all night, and when you wake up, the pain from your football injuries will be gone for good."

"For *good*, Doc?" Reggie asks, exchanging incredulous glances with his friends. If Dr. Saltzman can really get rid of their pain, he'll also be going a long way to reviving their aspirations of college and NFL football careers.

"For good," Saltzman beams. "Now go on; the nurse is waiting for you."

With renewed hope and vigor, the young men slip back out into the hallway, then hang an immediate right into the room next door. It is a large space with four beds, each attached to monitoring equipment, arranged in a semicircle around a central control desk where the data from each subject will be displayed and recorded minute by minute. The four football players nod in greeting to the nurse at the desk, then each claims a bed by placing his bag next to it.

Back in Dr. Saltzman's office, Colonel Bradley stares skeptically across the desk at his partner. "One night? What happened to the three months of testing? That's the data our sponsors want to see."

Saltzman gives him a slightly condescending smile. "I couldn't very well tell them that, could I? To them, it'll seem like they're headed for the overnight sleep you and I get. They'll wake up perfectly normal when we want them to."

"I hope so, Doctor, we're too close to fail now." Bradley pauses. "What's going to happen when they realize they've lost three months?"

Saltzman waves away his concern. "We'll cross that bridge when we come to it. However, I strongly suspect that when they wake up with no pain, they won't care."

CHAPTER 18
The Human Study Begins

"Now, boys, don't worry about all the monitors and beeping sounds. When I give you the signal, take three puffs of your inhaler. You'll go to sleep and, like I said, when you wake up, you'll be pain-free and free to resume pursuing your college football aspirations."

Reginald Doyo offers the doctor a brave smile then looks over to his three teammates. He can tell from the way their eyes are darting around that they're as nervous as he is. It's not the beds, which are elaborately cushioned and pneumatically controlled. They are quite comfortable, and the young athletes have no idea they are designed to prevent pressure sores that occur when a person lays in a static position for a long period of time. Numerous stickers have been placed on their chests, backs, and foreheads in order to monitor all body functions, including brain wave activity. But what bothers them the most are the catheters in their bladders and the never before experienced tingling sensation in their penises.

"Guys, this is what we agreed on," Reggie addresses them in the commanding voice of their team captain and unofficial leader, "and it's our best chance to play together again. Let's do it."

That's all they needed to hear. Each takes a deep breath as if preparing to dive under the water, then three puffs from their new inhalers as they were instructed. For the first five minutes, nothing seems to be happening except a tingling, half-numb sensation in their lips. Their accompanying anxiety is recorded at the center counsel monitoring station at the foot of the beds. The technician monitoring the readings looks up at Dr. Saltzman, who is intently watching the blood pressure, pulse rate, respiratory rate, and brain wave activity, all of which are much higher than normal. The technician shoots nervous glances at the doctor, but Saltzman's face is unreadable.

"Dr. Saltzman, their blood pressure is over two hundred. Should we stop and treat it?"

"No, not yet," Saltzman replies, still looking intently at the monitors. "The drug combination should be kicking in anytime now, and these are young healthy athletes. They can handle a short episode of hypertension and other physiological stresses. In fact, during their football games, they reach these same values and higher."

Then, as if on cue, the blood pressure, pulse and respiratory rates begin to down trend, and the nervous, rapid eye movements of the first five minutes are replaced with blank stares.

"There, the excitement is over," Saltzman says in a satisfied tone. "These vital signs will return to normal soon then should fall way below normal. I don't want you or any of the other techs to panic. The vital signs and brain activity will dip to scary low levels, but that's what we want. Remember, this is not sleep, it's hibernation."

***

On the same Monday morning, Detectives Molinaro and Ruiz are once again standing before Captain Russell. They don't need to see the tension in her jaw to know that things are bad; the most recent zombie murders on a college campus have significantly upped the ante on an already high profile case.

"You two better have something for me," Russell says, not bothering with the usual pleasantries. What is the point? She already knows how crappy their weekend was. "I've been screamed at by the mayor and a congresswoman, both of whom are being bombarded with calls from parents of college students in this city. I've also gotten several calls from—no surprise here—goddamned C.C. Murphy, who, among other things would like an exclusive with the two lead detectives on the case." The captain notes their wide eyes and emits a humorless laugh. "My first instinct of course was to tell her to go to hell, but you know it's only a matter of time before she speaks to the witness of the campus murders. I don't have to tell you how that interview will perpetuate the panic, especially if our side of the story isn't out there. For now, though, I put her off, said it would compromise an active investigation and that you're following some solid leads." She gives them a pointed look. "You are following some solid leads, aren't you?"

"We pretty much cleared Dr. Birnbaum at the psyche unit. The reports about the zombies don't really fit any known psychiatric diseases, including that 'walking corpse syndrome' Dr. Merriweather told us about. Also, the behavior of these zombies doesn't fit the known behaviors caused by street drugs, unless there's a new one out there that the toxicologists don't know anything about. Birnbaum is most likely just cruising toward retirement and leaves the unit to his charge nurses and orderlies. He's not hiding anything; he's just a burnout."

"Okay, Molinaro, that's what you *don't* have. Tell me what you do have."

"We now have four zombies—two white, two black. We have DNA on two of them. Neither is in the National DNA Database, which means they've never been arrested, applied for a government job, or been in the military. The good news is that there's a new DNA test that pinpointed their ethnic background for us."

"They can do that?"

Issy nods. "Yes, they can, and after a personal phone call from Dr. Merriweather, the top geneticist at the University of Miami ran the test for us." She pauses, excited to impart the knowledge they've gained as a result of her previous career. "Mitochondrial DNA is inherited from the mother and is therefore not shuffled by DNA from the father's side. This means it can be traced back many generations. The geneticist produced a statistical probability map that is ninety-three percent accurate."

Russell shakes her head as if to rid it of superfluous information. "Okay, okay, enough with the science bullshit. What do we know about the zombies?"

Andy pulls the geneticist's report from the pocket of his suit jacket. "I'm paraphrasing here," he announces. "The black man is originally of Western African origin, but his more recent DNA is from the Caribbean Basin, most likely Jamaica or Haiti. The white guy's heritage is from Western Europe, specifically today's Poland or the Czech Republic."

"That's all very interesting, Molinaro, but we still don't know who they are. At least we know they're not military, so I guess that rules out Colonel Bradley and your theory about post-traumatic stress disorder causing these guys to become zombies."

"Not exactly," Issy interjects. "Remember what we told you before? We're having him tailed, but in the meantime, we checked the airlines and found that he frequently flies into Newark and rents a car there. Yet he has no relatives or ex-wives there, and he doesn't check into any hotel in Newark or in New York City either. I would love to review his phone records."

"Not a chance, Issy. We don't have enough on him to subpoena his phone records, but I like the way you think. Good detective work often requires diligently following up on hunches. Continue to tail him. I want to know everywhere he goes and everyone he talks to." Just then, Russell's cell phone starts to ring. She glances down at it, frowns, and declines the call. "I've put extra people on this. No arguments, Molinaro, you two are still the lead investigators, but we need all hands on deck here. If we don't close this case soon, everyone from the governor to the guy who presses my uniforms will be demanding our resignations."

CHAPTER 19
Something Fishy

Tuesday finds Ruiz and Molinaro no closer to solving their case. For Dr. Merriweather, however, it is business as usual. He makes his noon hospital rounds with Dr. Glanville, Dr. Montel and two of his junior residents, all of whom are pleased to find that the two cancer patients and his jaw reconstruction patients from last Wednesday and Thursday are doing well enough to be discharged. Bevo St. Clair is also progressing well but has reported through Marle Celestine that he's in pain and feels his face is swollen. Merriweather's team has explained that this is to be expected just one day out from a twelve-hour surgery. They have also offered analgesics, but Mr. St. Clair has refused it each time. They explain, again through the interpreter, that he can relieve his discomfort with just the press of a button.

"Oh, he's knows," Marle tells them. "He just doesn't want it." She goes on to say that Bevo believes only in taking natural medicines and that those administered in the hospital are not natural. He will deal with the pain in his own way. Assured by normal blood tests and other signs that he is healing as anticipated, Merriweather and his team have little choice but to accept his wishes. After completing the onerous requirements of discharge orders and documentation for the other three patients, they head to the operating room for their afternoon surgery.

***

By four o'clock, the team has gathered in the recovery room, tired but pleased to have another successful surgery behind them. Drs. Glanville and Montel sit at neighboring computer stations, typing out postoperative orders and a short operative note, respectively, while Merriweather remains at the patient's bedside, describing the surgical findings to the family and reassuring them of their loved one's anticipated good outcome.

Their tasks are suddenly interrupted by the loud overhead speaker, "Code Blue, Room 318; Code Blue, Room 318..." The doctors' heads whip up. Code Blue indicates a dire, even life-threatening, event.

"That's Bevo St. Claire's room," Merriweather says. "Let's go." Without another word, the three of them jump up and rush for the nearest staircase.

"I found him unresponsive," the ward nurse announces when they get to the room. The code blue response team gets there at the same time, and the scene that follows has all the chaos and confusion of the latest medical TV drama.

"Get an AED," their leader barks out, "and start CPR."

Hearing the order, a member of the code blue team reflexively grabs the automatic electrical defibrillator, but before he can carry out the order, Merriweather stops them. "Wait a minute! He has a pulse, and a strong one at that. And he is also breathing."

The code blue team leader reiterates his order. "He's unresponsive, start CPR."

Dr. Merriweather glares sternly at him, and a standoff begins.

"What the hell are chest compressions going to do for a man with a pulse? You can't breathe for him any better than he's breathing for himself." Dr. Merriweather presses St. Claire's thumb nail to push the blood out of the nail bed. After releasing his pressure, the white nail bed pinks up in two seconds. "See, the blanching refills in two seconds or less. Tissues are perfusing. Something else is going on here."

By this time, Drs. Glanville and Montel have hooked up the AED. Sure enough, the cardiogram tracing is normal. "No shockable rhythm detected," announces the devices' robotic voice. Everyone except Merriweather exchanges puzzled glances, and even the code blue team leader concedes that there is no need for a resuscitation.

As the chaos subsides, Dr. Merriweather calls for a formal twelve-lead electrocardiogram and instructs the nurse to call Marle Celestine.

"You don't need her," she replies. "Mr. St. Claire is in a coma. He can't talk."

Normally, this response would not ruffle Merriweather. But after dealing with the code blue team leader's inappropriate snap decisions, he's in no mood for push back.

"Goddammit, Esther, just do it." Marle Celestine knows the Haitian culture backward and forward; she lived there. "I need to talk to her now. Also, get the blood tubes for us. I'll call neurology to get the EEG. We need to ask them to rule out a stroke."

Esther rushes off, smarting from Dr. Merriweather's rebuke, while Drs. Glanville and Montel immediately look for local nerve deficits such as one-sided facial paralysis, or the tongue pulled to one side—anything that might indicate a stroke. Finding nothing, they then check basic nerve reflexes and again find normal responses.

"No signs of a stroke, Dr. Merriweather," they blurt out almost in unison.

"I didn't really expect to find any," he replies as he takes a seat next to St. Claire's bed. "This is similar to the kind of drug-induced coma the neurosurgeons use to limit brain swelling in closed head injuries." Sighing, he folds his hands across his chest, trying to figure out why a person with a completely normal examination would be in an apparent coma. "Something funny is going on here." He's spends another five minutes considering the matter, then his train of thought is interrupted by a hand on his shoulder. He looks up to see Marle Celestine standing beside him.

"Dr. Merriweather, what's happened to Mr. St. Clair?"

"I really don't know, Marle, maybe you can tell me. When we were talking to him about his pain this morning, did he say anything else?"

She shakes her head. "Just that he would deal with the pain himself, as his father taught him."

"Well, what the hell did his father teach him?"

Marle falls silent for a moment, and just when Merriweather thinks they've hit another dead end, she says, "You know, his father was a tribal voodoo shaman. He dealt with pain or bad social situations by putting himself or others who came to him in a trance."

Merriweather enjoys a moment of comic relief. "Oh, come on now, Marle," he chuckles, "you don't expect me to believe Bevo put himself into a trance so deep that a whole code blue team barking orders and placing a defibrillator and EKG pads on him, even sticking him with needles didn't wake him? I mean, he didn't even blink once!"

Merle gives him a gentle smile. "Dr. Merriweather, you don't understand voodoo. The power of the mind can be very strong."

Still highly skeptical, Dr. Merriweather swallows a retort so as not to offend Ms. Celestine. He looks back at Bevo and notices for the first time a half-empty glass of water from the table beside the bed.

Almost without thinking, he reaches for the glass and brings it up to his nose. "Ugh," he exclaims as he draws back, "that smells like dead fish."

He holds the glass up to Marle, who also grimaces at the horribly pungent odor. "Voodoo shamans often give potions to their clients and to themselves. Do you think it's possible Mr. St. Clair took such a potion?"

"I believe that more than I believe in self-induced trances, Marle. I'll have this water analyzed for drugs, and in the meantime, let's look through his personal belongings. It may be an invasion of privacy, but if it gives us a clue as to how to help him, it's well worth it."

It doesn't take long for Dr. Merriweather and Marle to find a small, clear jar containing a dry, gray granular material.

"Do you think this is it?" Marle asks.

"We'll soon see." Merriweather unscrews the lid. Immediately, they draw back in disgust as the same dead fish smell floods their nostrils.

"Ms. Celestine," he says, "I believe we've discovered the source of Bevo's 'coma'."

CHAPTER 20
Something Fishy Part II

It's Thursday, eleven days after the early morning demise of Chester Bland that began the zombie murder panic. In Key West, Danny the dockhand awakes, confused and disoriented, from his apparent coma.

"What happened?" he asks, staring groggily at the relieved but puzzled doctors at his bedside.

"You're in the hospital, Danny. What is the last thing you remember?"

"Only the worst pain in my life! Boy, am I glad that's over."

In Room 318 at Dade South Hospital, Bevo St. Claire also awakens from his deep slumber, completely free of pain. He learned from his shaman father to combine certain natural ingredients that would make him sleep and prevent pain demons from getting into his mind. This particular potion consists of dried calabash and mango rind together with dried and ground sea turtle skin. However, the main ingredient—and the one responsible for the pungent odor—is dried and powdered puffer fish skin. Bevo knew full well that the dose he took would last about two days, long enough to defeat the pain demons.

Dr. Merriweather is thrilled when, upon arriving at the hospital, he hears the good news about Bevo. When he later gets a call that Danny is also awake and seemingly in good health, he considers it a happy, if perplexing, coincidence.

As soon as he has a free minute, he calls Dr. George Irvin, Director of the forensic section of the medical examiner's office.

"George, any results on the powder and water I sent you the other day?"

"Yeah, where the hell did you get this concoction?"

"My patient from Haiti took it, and it put him to sleep. He woke up just this morning."

"Well, he's lucky it didn't kill him. First, the stuff in the water is the same as the powder. He probably mixed it with water to get it by his nose. The powder contains some fruit residue with nothing harmful in it, but the main ingredient is tetrodotoxin, which can be deadly."

"Tetrodotoxin!" Dr. Merriweather exclaims. "From *puffer fish*?"

"You know about this stuff, Merriweather?"

"Of course. Most tropical water fishermen and skin divers know of it. Since this guy is from Haiti, he probably used the Caribbean-Atlantic species of puffer fish. The toxin from the Indo-Pacific species is much more deadly. As a matter of fact, chefs in Japan must be specifically certified in the cleaning and preparation of puffer fish before they can serve it to the public. They're called Fugu chefs after the Japanese local name for the puffer fish. Both puffer fish contain a similar neurotoxin, but the Caribbean-Atlantic one is much less concentrated."

"Well, that explains why your patient survived," Dr. Irvin chuckles. "Next time, tell him to take an Ambien."

***

"Chief, we have to talk about Colonel Bradley. His military record is dotted with Article Fifteen reprimands, investigations, and even a court martial in which he was found not guilty. But, well, let's just say doubts linger." Issy pauses, half-expecting Russell to cut her off for bringing up useless information.

"Go on, Ruiz. Just because there've been no zombie murders reported this week doesn't necessarily mean we've seen the last of them, and we're no closer to an arrest. If you got something on Bradley, let's hear it."

"It seems Colonel Bradley has always been a schemer and was caught in several get-rich-quick ventures. In his first one, he organized a base-wide betting ring. He took bets on college and pro football games, horse races, dog races, boxing matches, and so on. Of course he took a commission on each bet as well as a percentage of any winnings."

"Okay…" Russell replies, and Issy can tell her interest is waning, "…but this is relatively minor stuff."

"Sure, at first," Issy says, "but his next escapade involved attempting to sell military scrap and even a decommissioned PT boat to Bolivia, supposedly for their use against drug runners. Turns out he was actually trying to sell it *to* the drug runners. There wasn't enough evidence for jail or even a dishonorable discharge, but he was demoted one rank. He's actually a lieutenant colonel, not a full colonel."

"Okay, I'm still wondering how this is related to the zombie murders, but first let's go back to the court martial...."

Issy feels Molinaro's stare and knows he's trying to gauge whether she is impressing the chief or annoying her.

"That's where my suspicion comes in," she says. "He was accused of giving the Marines under his command performance-enhancing drugs without their permission. The theory was that he was trying to make them into 'super soldiers' on par with the Navy Seals and the Army Rangers so he could command his own elite covert team. Apparently, he was never satisfied with being a battlefield surgeon; he dreamed of leading a combat troop. He would've been convicted too, but apparently his men were too scared to testify because of some connections he had. The high command made him a deal—an honorable discharge with full benefits in exchange for him leaving active duty and taking up a medical command position in a veteran's hospital. They also promised that the court martial would not appear on his record. Needless to say, he took the deal."

Russell shakes her head in disgust. "That's why the FBI couldn't find any of this." She pauses to give Issy a curious look. "So tell me, Ruiz, how did you?"

Issy glances from Chief Russell to Molinaro and back again. "Uh, actually, I got my sources from my ex-husband. He has a few friends in the military and helped me find the right people to talk to, but it took some persuading and only after I promised it would be completely off the record."

Chief Russell sees the look of surprise cross Molinaro's face. *So, he didn't know she spoke to her ex ...* She files this potential conflict away to be discussed after the case is closed.

"So you think Bradley's experience in drugging his own troops is somehow connected to our zombie murders?"

"Absolutely. From the beginning, Dr. Merriweather has believed the zombies' behavior seemed drug-induced. Eyewitness accounts of this behavior have been consistent—that includes the statements from the girl who saw last Friday's campus murders. Also, Colonel Bradley was evasive when Andy and I questioned him, not to mention that his military record illustrates a pattern of behavior that I don't think stopped with his discharge from active duty."

"I can't believe you didn't tell me about any of this," Molinaro mutters.

"Well, I know how you feel about him, and before I upset you, I just wanted to make sure the information was worth it...."

"But how is this going to work if—"

"We don't have time for lovers' quarrels," the Chief snaps.

"Andy, a girl must do what a girl must do. Deal with it. This is our best lead yet. Let's put some pressure on the good Colonel."

CHAPTER 21
The Makings of a Zombie

Dr. Merriweather spends most of Friday immersed in writing a paper on his team's stem cell studies. He welcomes the short respite from his hectic surgical schedule; unfortunately, the relative downtime allows concern about his future with Heather to creep into his mind. Several times, he finds himself reaching for his cell phone, only to pause, his hand hovering over the device like a conflicted teen.

He hasn't felt this way since he tried to get up the courage to call Joan Hugen and ask her to the prom. That was thirty-eight years ago, and the memory of it reminds Merriweather why he's always considered nostalgia to be a useless emotion. What he can't figure out is why he's so nervous about calling Heather now. They've always talked through their problems.

"This is different," he says out loud.

"You need something, Dr. Merriweather?" Mishy calls from the outer office.

"Uh, no, Mishy. I'm fine."

But he isn't fine. His relationship with Heather has never

faced this sort of challenge before. Sure, they've gone through relatively rough patches, when the demands of careers, or, in her case, two young sons, made the distance between them seem more than physical; however, their commitment to each other was never in doubt. This is different. Standing her up for an entire weekend to go diving, even if it did have a noble medical purpose, was inexcusable. Almost worse was that, he forgot about it altogether, and that, coupled with the string of previous plans he'd cancelled, well, that added up to a deal-breaker.

Merriweather realizes he got up from his chair and is pacing the office. *This is ridiculous.* He picks up the phone and dials her cell. After six rings, he hears Heather's almost chipper voicemail greeting.

Merriweather debates for a moment then hangs up without leaving a message. *Maybe she's in the middle of something and couldn't answer,* he tells himself, *or, more likely, she probably saw that it was me.*

He's never been one to second-guess himself, yet, since the night of their fight, it seems all the things that he should have said and done differently have been running on a loop in his mind. "Enough is enough," he says, forcing himself to snap out of his preoccupation and concentrate on the two-day coma episodes of dockhand Danny and Bevo St. Clair. *What are the chances,* he thinks as he returns to his desk, *that two outwardly similar cases were caused by two different fish toxins?* What perplexes him most is the fact that both men woke up perfectly normal, with no memory of anything.

Drs. Glanville and Montel also take advantage of the rare

lull in action by organizing an impromptu party at Dr. Glanville's home that evening. They even extend invitations to the resident staff at the three other hospitals.

At eight p.m. sharp, Luke Young pulls into the parking space just below the stairwell to Michele Ruiz's second-floor apartment. A moment later, he stares appreciatively as Mishy, dressed in tight-fitting jeans and a halter top that shows off her ample chest, bounds down the stairway. Her raven-black hair flows down her back, and as she slides into the passenger seat, Luke inhales the sweet scent of coconut shampoo. She leans toward him, and as their lips meet, she feels Luke's hand at her waist, then move upward toward her breast.

"Now, now," she says as she playfully swats his hand away, "there'll be time for that later." She rubs his arm affectionately. "You've all been going balls to the wall for months. You need a night to relax."

"I know a way to relax..." Luke gives her a seductive look. "Okay, okay, you're right. It'll be nice to hang with everyone. There'll certainly be no time for parties once I start with the main anesthesia service next month. You know I want to develop a facial pain treatment center when I graduate," he says, his face, voice and demeanor now expressing a very different type of passion. "So this month learning pain control and pain management under Dr. Saltzman is invaluable." He flashes a grin at Mishy. "Boy, do I owe Dr. Merriweather for that one!"

"That's just like Merriweather," she says. "My mom always told me, if you work hard and he believes in you, there's nothing he won't do to help."

"Well, she's right, and I'll never forget this."

"So how was your first week with Saltzman?"

"Oh, Mishy, this is really what I want to do. It's fantastic. You should see the layout Dr. Saltzman has. He's doing some really advanced research in pain control. I've seen him give injections that have stopped people's chronic leg pain instantly, and he has these inhalers that literally stop migraines in their tracks. In fact, he has different inhalers for every different sort of pain: neck pain, back pain, pain on urination and even tooth pain. Can you imagine an oral and maxillofacial surgeon like me being able to take away a toothache and/or surgical pain with just a few puffs?"

"That sounds incredible, Luke." Mishy gives him a sideways glance. "I've never seen you so enthused before. Should I be jealous?"

Luke wiggles an eyebrow at her. "Not at all, but I do wish I could spend more time with him. He's a real genius. Maybe I can talk Dr. Merriweather into a few more months during my senior year."

By nine o'clock, the party at Glanville's rented three-bedroom house in the Kendall Lakes area of West Miami is in full swing. The strong bond among the surgical residents, developed through long hours of working side by side in challenging situations, translates well into the festive atmosphere. Aside from the most amusing anecdotes, they keep shoptalk to a minimum so as to include their significant others in the conversation.

"Anyone for margaritas?" Dr. Glanville calls out. "Or should I say, anyone who is not on call?"

His question is greeted with a mix of groans and requests for the delicious cocktail. After filling several orders— rocks or straight, salt or no salt, depending on personal preference—Glanville mingles among his guests to make sure everyone is having a good time. As he gets close to his own bedroom, the familiar scent of pot suddenly floods his nostrils. Opening the door, he finds two of the first-year residents sitting by an open window, passing a half-smoked joint between them.

"Jeff, Seth … really?"

In their nervousness, Seth jumps back as if scalded while Jeff drops the joint out the window.

"Shit, sorry, Dr. Glanville.…"

"You should be sorry, but not as sorry as you'll be if Mer-riweather ever finds out. You know how he feels about this kind of stuff—he'd kick your butts and then kick you both right out of this program."

The two nod furiously, terrified at the mere mention of Merriweather. "You're not going to tell him, are you?"

Glanville narrows his eyes at them. "Not tonight," he says finally, "but if I ever catch you doing this shit again, calling Dr. Merriweather is going to be first on my very long to-do list."

"Thanks, man," Jeff says. "Really, I mean—"

"Don't thank me," Glanville says as he heads for the door, "just go wash up. You two stink."

By eleven p.m., cocktails have been replaced by coffee, and talk has turned to the residents' plans for the future. Some plan to enter a private practice, some hope to land a position in a teaching program; all are confident that the program's stellar reputation and, more importantly, Dr. Merriweather's support will open doors for them. One or two want more than anything to replace Dr. Glanville as Dr. Merriweather's fellow and work closely with him on his research projects.

Suddenly, the conversation is abruptly shattered by a loud cry of pain. Everyone looks over to see senior resident Dr. Montel doubling over. Immediately, a few of the residents jump up and help him over to the sofa, where he curls up in a fetal position. Dr. Glanville rushes to his side.

"David, what's the matter?"

"It's my kidney stone," he gasps. "I've had it for months."

"Dave, we need to take you to the emergency room."

"No, no, no, don't do that. I'll be alright. The pain will go away. It always does." Just then, Montel is gripped by another wave of agony. His forehead beaded with sweat, he curls up even more, yet still he continues to resist his colleagues' offer to take him to an emergency room.

"Dave, come on now. Be a patient not a doctor. If you haven't passed this stone in the past couple of months, it's not likely to pass now, and your pain could last for hours."

Luke Young breaks through the crowd of fellow residents hovering over their stricken colleague. "Hey, I got one of Dr. Saltzman's pain inhalers out in the car. It's amazing stuff, knocks out pain in three puffs."

Dave Montel is about to refuse when yet another wave of severe pain courses through his abdomen and back. "Okay," he squeaks out, "let me try it."

Luke dashes out the door and returns a moment later with an inhaler in his hand. "This is a leftover. Dr. Saltzman's using a newer formulation on four guys in his research study, but it's half full and still potent."

Glanville and the others exchange dubious glances as he hands the inhaler to Montel. Although they have heard about Dr. Saltzman's groundbreaking work, it is difficult to believe Luke's claims. Their doubt turns to amazement, however, when after taking just three puffs and deeply inhaling the vapor, Montel relaxes and uncurls from his fetal position. "Oh my God," he says weakly but clearly more comfortable than he was a minute ago, "it worked! The pain is gone."

Glanville, however, has learned from Dr. Merriweather to be skeptical of such dramatic results, especially after observing them just once. "Dave, are you sure you just didn't pass that stone?"

"I don't know, James. I only know the pain is completely gone."

"Come on, guys," Glanville says, "let's give him some space."

The crowd slowly disperses, leaving David Montel, now joined on the sofa by his wife Carol, to recover from the episode.

Ten minutes later, Glanville circles back to check on his friend.

"David," he hears Montel's wife say, "are you listening to me?"

David does not respond, just stares straight ahead with unblinking eyes.

"Come on, David." She stands and holds out a hand to him. "You've had a busy week, and you're exhausted from that kidney stone pain. Let's go home now."

Without uttering a word, Montel accepts her hand, stands up and heads toward the front door. From a few feet away, Glanville notes his colleague's fixed gaze and short, shuffling steps that are completely different from his usual strong, determined gait.

He is not the only one who notices Montel's uncharacteristic behavior. Seth, one of the two pot smoking residents, moves into his path with cell phone in hand. His goal: to get a photo of the "drunk" senior resident.

A second after the flash of the camera goes off, the usually affable David Montel drops Carol's hand and lunges forward, grabbing Seth by the throat.

"David, no!" his wife screams as Glanville rushes over and tries, unsuccessfully, to pull Montel off the gasping Seth.

"Somebody get over here!" Glanville shouts. Immediately, Luke Young and the other residents jump in and attempt to overpower Montel. It takes several minutes and four men to pin him down. Through it all, David Montel remains staring straight ahead, seemingly unaware of his surroundings or of his wife, who's sobbing by his side.

"Someone call 911," Glanville barks to Jeff, who immediately pulls out his cell.

A few minutes later, the fire rescue truck pulls up in front of the house. Now completely docile, Montel allows himself to be strapped to a stretcher.

"It's going to be okay, buddy," Glanville tells him then turns to one of the responders. "Take him to Dade South Hospital. I will pay the difference."

A few feet away, a shocked and devastated Luke Young watches his colleague disappear into the ambulance.

"I don't understand," he whispers to Mishy. "Can this be from the inhaler? If so, I—"

She cuts him off with a gentle squeeze of his hand. "You can't blame yourself. We don't even know what caused this yet. We'll talk to Dr. Merriweather."

Luke nods, though he fears Merriweather's disapproval more than anything.

CHAPTER 22
The March to the Nobel Prize

Dr. Merriweather arrives at the Dade South intensive care unit amid monitors sounding off a steady slow beat and flashing low but acceptable numbers. Montel is in stable condition, but this does little to assuage the worries of his wife and fellow residents. Joining them at his bedside is internal medicine specialist Orlando Rodriquez. Merriweather passes by Dr. Rodriguez and goes directly to Dr. Montel's wife.

"Carol," he says, pulling her into a hug, "I'm so sorry to hear this. What happened?"

She wipes her eyes as the two step away to talk. "I don't know. After the pain went away, we talked for about two minutes or so, then I noticed the blank stare. He didn't even seem to understand a word I said, but I thought he was just exhausted from fighting off the pain from his kidney stone. I took him by the hand to lead him out to our car, and that's when the flash from the cell phone camera went off." New tears spring to her eyes. "He became agitated and lost control...."

"Okay," he says, placing a tender hand on Carol's back to guide her back to her husband's bedside, "we'll get to the bottom of this."

He then motions for Drs. Glanville and Rodriguez to follow him over to an adjacent empty ICU bay. "Orlando, what do you make of this?"

"I don't know much," the internist replies. "He's in some type of catatonic state, probably drug-related."

"I've known David now for almost five years. I never figured him to be a drug user."

Dr. Glanville breaks in. "I've known Dave for four years, and I know he doesn't use drugs, never has. This may be due to the pain medication Luke gave him for the kidney stone."

"Kidney stone? Pain medication?"

"Yes, apparently he's had the stone for a while, and the pain flared up during the party. He was doubled over but refused our offer to bring him here to the emergency room. The pain got more and more intense, so Luke gave him three puffs of some pain formula he got from Dr. Saltzman's lab."

"Pain medicine from an inhaler ... I've never heard of such a thing. Have you, Orlando?"

"No, there are none on the market that I know about, but we should do a complete tox screen on him to check it out."

"Where is this inhaler anyhow?" barks Dr. Merriweather, not even attempting to disguise his anger.

Dr. Glanville walks back to the small crowd of residents hovering around David Montel's bed and asks Luke Young to follow him.

"Luke, do you still have the inhaler you used on Dave?"

A flash of panic crosses his face. "Yes, Dr. Merriweather, it's right here." He reaches into the pocket of his trousers, pulls out the inhaler and hands it over. "I didn't know this would happen, really. I was only trying to help Dave out of his pain. This stuff worked so well with Saltzman's patients. I had no idea...."

"That's okay," Merriweather says in a softer tone, "just think back to what patients used this stuff before."

"I don't know that either. It may have been one of the four football guys he's using in his sleep study lab."

Merriweather raises an eyebrow at him. "*Sleep study?* Jake Saltzman is not into sleep disorders or obstructive sleep apnea." He grows pensive for a long moment then says, "I've got a hunch, Luke. Can you get into his sleep lab and take a DNA sample from these four guys?" Without waiting for an answer, he adds, "I'm going to give you four DNA swab kits. Swab the cheek mucosa of each of these football guys, and get them to me ASAP. I'll run it by our geneticist."

Merriweather pauses for another moment as he weighs his words. Something is tugging at the back of his mind. "Luke, I hesitate to ask you this, but look around Saltzman's lab. See if there's anything about these pain medications that can help us understand what happened to Dr. Montel."

"Well, one thing's for sure," Orlando says, eyeing the inhaler, "we need to analyze whatever's in that."

"You're right. I'll get my buddy George Irvin over at the medical examiner's office to analyze it right away. Heck, I just had him look into a Haitian voodoo potion. He's going to either love me or hate me for this one."

***

That same night, while Merriweather and his team try to figure out what really happened to Dr. Montel, Colonel Bradley pays a visit to Dr. Saltzman's lab. As usual, his saunter and smirk project an air of self-assuredness bordering on arrogance.

"Okay, Saltzman, you wanted to see me. What you got?"

"You said you're going to visit our sponsor tomorrow, right? Well look at this."

Dr. Saltzman leads Colonel Bradley into the bay where the four former high school football stars are lying quietly on their respective beds, as they have been for the past five days.

"What do you notice, Colonel?"

Bradley studies them for a moment. "Well, they have no IVs, no feeding tubes. They're just lying there."

"Yes, but is that all you notice? Look at the monitors, Colonel."

Bradley takes a moment to scan the monitors. He takes several minutes to comprehend what he is seeing and remains quizzical about the values in front of him. "Are these monitors working? Has something gone wrong here?"

Saltzman turns to him, eyes bright with excitement. "No, no, my good Colonel. In fact, everything is going perfectly. This is the first bit of proof I want you to take to our sponsors. Here are some photographs of these subjects and their monitors. Notice the pulse is one or two beats per minute, the respiratory rate is one per minute and the blood pressure is sixty over forty. What you're looking at, Colonel, is not a coma. It's not even hibernation. It's *suspended animation.* The careful balancing of the doses of my three centennial ingredients has achieved what was thought to be impossible. I'm sure we can maintain this state for the three months our sponsors require, maybe even much longer. That should impress them enough to validate their donation for this research center, and of course their support of my Nobel Prize, don't you think?" Saltzman finishes with his arms across his chest in a triumphant pose.

A grin splitting his face, the Colonel glances from Saltzman to their subjects. "Holy shit, Saltzman, you did it. You really did it, and all with just inhalers that one can self-administer. This will be the medical find of the century!"

Dr. Saltzman offers him a smug smile. "Indeed, it will be."

A few minutes later, Colonel Bradley is still wearing a small, satisfied smile as he leaves the building and heads for his metallic blue jaguar. He passes within just twenty feet of the black Lincoln MKZ in which Andy Molinaro and Issy are seated. Issy notes his time of leaving while Andy snaps numerous high-speed photographs, some of which zoom in on the photographic prints Bradley carries in his hand.

Issy stifles a yawn. "I need coffee."

"You're right," he says excitedly, "Bradley is up to something. But why's he going to Dr. Saltzman's lab at this time of night? Isn't Dr. Saltzman one of Merriweather's friends, and isn't he pretty much a straight shooter?" He pauses. "Do you think Colonel Bradley is extorting Saltzman?"

"I don't know, Andy. I was wondering that myself. I'm calling Dr. Merriweather now."

Dr. Merriweather's cell phone rings while he is finishing his own examination of the zombie-like appearance and behavior of his chief resident.

"Yes, Issy, what's up?"

"Hey Chief," she says, not bothering to ask why he's up so late. "Andy and I tailed Colonel Bradley from the VA over to Dr. Saltzman's lab at the Life Sciences Center. Turns out Bradley's military career is checkered with devious schemes, not the least of which is doping his platoon members. We're wondering if he may be extorting Saltzman to get some drugs for his PTSD patients, or even worse. What do you know about Dr. Saltzman?"

"We knew each other as residents and kept in occasional contact over the years. He's driven, he's brilliant and wants to be known for his brilliance. He has a big ego but one that he's earned…" Merriweather pauses. "Funny you mention him now."

"Why's that funny?"

"Well, I'm actually up in the ICU with Dave Montel. He apparently was given three puffs of a pain-killing formulation of Dr. Saltzman's, which turned him into—forgive me for saying this—'a zombie'. I'm actually looking at him now. He doesn't respond to my voice or pinching him. He doesn't even feel a needle stick, and his eyes are open with a blank stare. His blood pressure and pulse are low but not dangerously so. I hate to say it, but I'm worried my old friend is possibly being used or drawn into something by this Bradley. In any event, I'm having the contents of the inhaler tested. I should have some results for you in a day or two."

"Great info, Chief. Andy and I will continue tailing Bradley. We'll have another unit stake out Saltzman's lab. As of yet, we don't have enough probable cause to get a subpoena to search his lab, and..." Issy pauses. "I know I'm asking a lot, but maybe you could visit him for us and get an idea of what may be going on there. Can you do it for me, Chief?"

"No need to beg, Issy. I'm as curious as you and even more concerned that my old friend has gotten in over his head."

CHAPTER 23
The Meeting

Ten-thirty Saturday morning, Colonel Bradley's flight touches down at Newark International Airport. As usual, he has traveled light, with just a small duffle bag he shoves in the overhead bin. After leaving the plane, he heads directly for the National Rental Car desk by the baggage claim. Twenty minutes later, he drives the black luxury sedan off the lot and joins the flow of traffic exiting the airport. As he merges onto Route I-78, the traffic is unusually light. Although Bradley is not one for superstition, he takes this as positive omen that his business dealings will go smoothly as well. He turns on the radio and follows the signs for Route 24 West, unaware of the silver, rather nondescript car following him.

Twenty-six miles and twenty minutes later, he arrives at the Morris Plains headquarters of Apollo Drug Company. He pulls up to the main security gate and brusquely hands his driver's license to the guard.

"I'm here to see David Steiner," he announces in a tone one would use with a servant.

With a barely concealed eye-roll, the guard picks up the phone and, after a brief exchange, returns Colonel

Bradley's identification and directs him to the parking area for VIP visitors.

"You'll find Mr. Steiner's office on the second floor," he says, pushing a button to open the gate. "Have a good day, sir," he adds, but the colonel has already closed the car window.

After parking the car, Bradley digs around in his duffle bag and pulls out a manilla envelope. It's a grey and drizzly day, and as he crosses the parking lot, he resists the urge to cover his head with it. Once inside the building, he heads without hesitation toward the nearest elevator bank. The directions to David Steiner's office were unnecessary as Colonel Bradley, a frequent visitor, knows all too well the location of nearly all the executive offices on the second floor.

The elevator doors open onto the spacious, marble-floored outer reception area. Bradley passes by the empty secretary's desk and strides purposefully to the CEO's plush office. He finds David Steiner, a slightly built, clean-shaven man in his late forties, sitting behind a surprisingly modest desk. To his right stands another man around the same age, his blue eyes coldly flicking over the colonel. Instead of their usual expensive suits, both are dressed in Saturday attire of khaki slacks and light-colored blue button-down shirts.

Leaning back casually, David Steiner announces, "George, welcome back. You've met my Marketing Director, Steve Bloom, before. I've asked him to join us today."

Steiner motions to a plush leather chair in front of his desk. "Have a seat. How about a little drink? I know it's still morning, but if your phone call was any indication, we have some celebrating to do." With that, he puts his feet up on the desk as if in anticipation of good news.

Colonel Bradley waves away the offer of a drink. "David, you're going to like this..." he begins as he takes a seat. "Old Saltzman has done it." He opens the envelope, slides out several papers, then reaches over to place them on the desk in front of Steiner.

With Bloom hanging over his shoulder, Steiner picks up the papers and begins shuffling through them.

"You'll see," Colonel Bradley says, "that the four subjects are fast asleep with no perceptible pulse, few respirations, a low blood pressure but one sustainable of life with a greatly reduced metabolic need. Gentlemen, this is what we've been looking for—suspended animation."

Steiner examines several photos of the four football players with monitors of each clearly visible, confirming the obtunded vital signs. He then moves on to the metabolic data sheets. With his feet now off the desk and firmly planted on the floor, his finger goes over each day's weight, urine output and any bowel movement excrement. After a long moment, he gives Bloom a nod of confirmation then turns to Bradley with a rare look of astonishment.

"Steve, this is incredible. After one week, no weight loss, only five milliliters of urine, and no appreciable bowel movements. If this one-week data holds up, it means Saltzman has succeeded in nearly stopping the aging process. Do you know what this could mean?"

"I do," Steve Bloom says smoothly, "it means it's a blockbuster multibillion—even trillion—dollar item. It means we'll sell it to NASA at a premium price for their nine-month manned mission to Mars, and who knows where after that. It also means it's possible to go to sleep and wake up at some point in a presumably better future, whether it's simply to witness that future or to take advantage of a newfound cure for whatever ails them. My survey indicated that people will pay anything for such a thing."

"Whatever else it is, George, it's well worth your project leader fee and the money we sunk into Saltzman's lab." Steiner claps his hands together. "Gentlemen, I'd say it's time for that drink."

He springs to his feet and walks over to the bar in the corner, where a bottle of eighteen-year-old single malt Glenfiddich is waiting. He pours three glasses and carries them back to his desk, where they ceremoniously clink their glasses together.

Bradley is still savoring that first smooth sip when Steiner asks, "George, can you trust Saltzman to keep on this project until its completion, and keep it under wraps?"

"Oh, Dr. Saltzman will *certainly* remain focused on this project. Remember, this guy is all about the recognition. He's hoping your influence in Europe will get him a nomination from the Nobel Prize Committee." Bradley pauses to take another sip of scotch. "About keeping it quiet, I'm not so sure. That same desire for recognition means he's always dying to blurt it out to one of his buddies, especially that Dr. Merriweather."

Steiner's smile twists into a grimace. "Dr. *Robert* Merriweather?"

"You've got to be kidding me," Bloom growls.

"Yeah, Dr. Robert Merriweather..." Bradley says, perplexed. "What's the problem?"

"The problem, Colonel Bradley, is that Dr. Merriweather is responsible for costing this company billions of dollars. You've heard of the Bone Protect case?"

"He's *that* guy?" Bradley asks, visibly paling.

Last year, Merriweather exposed Apollo's cover-up of the dead jaw bone complication arising from the use of Bone Protect, a much-touted, very lucrative drug prescribed for osteoporosis. His testimony in a Manhattan courtroom won the case for the plaintiffs; it also nearly cost him his life when Apollo's lead attorney put out a hit on him. Thanks to Andy Molinaro, his then-partner Enrique Gonzalez, and a little bit of luck, Merriweather survived to tell the tale. Now, it looks like he might also pose a threat to Steiner's latest venture.

"We need to make it clear to Saltzman that he keeps this under wraps, and it needs to happen immediately." Steiner picks up his cell phone and quickly checks his calendar. "Set up a meeting for this Friday."

"Sure will, David," Bradley smiles, hoping to lighten the mood and shift the focus back to the good news he delivered. "It's all part of my project leadership fee. Speaking of which, I believe it's time for an installment, given how far I've advanced the project thus far."

"Yes, yes, of course." Steiner gestures vaguely to an area behind the colonel. "In the briefcase, two-point-five million—same as last time. You'll get the final payment when we patent Saltzman's formula."

"Excellent." Bradley finishes his drink then rises from his chair and goes to collect his prize. "It's been a pleasure doing business with you, gentlemen."

"You don't have to rush off, George...."

"Actually, I have business to attend to back in Florida." He eyes the humidor on Steiner's desk. "I will, however, help myself to one of these." Colonel Bradley plucks a Cuban Cohiba from the humidor, lights it, and exhales a thick puff of smoke.

When he reaches the door, he turns to give Steiner and Bloom a half salute. "Again, it's been a pleasure. I'll be in touch about the meeting with Saltzman."

As he exits the building, briefcase in one hand and cigar in the other, Colonel Bradley allows himself a chuckle. Turns out a hotshot CEO and a world-class doctor are no different than anyone else; they needed to be handled with just the right combination of kiss-ass and confidence. It wouldn't be hard to convince Saltzman not to open his big mouth to Merriweather. Bradley is still smiling as he tosses the briefcase into the car, unaware of the binoculars fixed on him.

As the colonel pulls out of the lot, Detective Greg Taft from the Newark Police Department sets the binoculars on the seat next to him and picks up his cell phone to call

Andy Molinaro. Back in the day, he and Molinaro served in the same unit at the FBI and were frequent workout partners at the gym.

"Hey, Andy, it's me. Your friend Colonel Bradley just paid a visit to Apollo Headquarters. Yeah, in Morris Plains. Seems like he paid a visit to the big boys. The only cars here are in the spots reserved for the CEO and the Marketing Director, and Bradley left with a cigar and a briefcase he didn't have when he entered. Yeah, okay, buddy, I'll let you know where he goes. I suspect it'll be the airport."

CHAPTER 24
The Witch's Brew

Over the next week, Dr. Jake Saltzman intently monitors his four subjects and is pleased when they show no changes in weight and no real output of bodily functions. Their vital signs remain stable but almost imperceptible except by the sophisticated monitoring devices being used. Indeed, the casual observer would fear that they were not alive. Although it is not a complete suspension of bodily metabolism and function, it is a true one, sufficient to keep people in this condition for years, perhaps even decades. Certainly, it would last the ambitious eighteen-month voyage to Mars and back planned by NASA once the political will and funding favor it.

Dr. Saltzman looks forward to the successful three-month completion of the study, soon to be followed by an announcement to the world. The accolades and respect that he will surely get from his colleagues, not to mention his likely Nobel Prize nomination, will finally make all the years of sacrifice worth it. The brilliant scientist, once revered by Merriweather and others for his dedication to the betterment of humanity, is now driven solely by ego and personal goals.

At Apollo Drug Company, David Steiner and Steve Bloom envision an entirely different scenario—one of commercial applications and obscene profits to be gained by Saltzman's breakthrough. The two spend much of the week going over the potential markets of a so-called "long sleep" drug and respective revenues to be anticipated by them. Like Saltzman, their first goal is to get NASA to test it out and use it for their Mars Manned Mission project. The groundwork for this has already been set by David Steiner's numerous visits to Cape Canaveral as well as the NASA headquarters in Houston. His generous corporate donations to their space station project, as well as discounted and even free Apollo drugs to their healthcare plans, has generated what Steiner likes to refer to as a fair amount of "good will". In other words, one hand washes the other.

After NASA, he plans to market the product to special long-term sleep clinics for people with chronic or life-threatening disease for which cures are within a decade or two away. They know of course that no insurance company or Medicare will cover this type of therapy. It will be available only to those who can afford it.

"What do you think we should charge, Steve?" opens the CEO. The two are sitting in Steiner's office, each sipping on two fingers of Glenfiddich.

"I dunno, Dave," Bloom says with a shrug. "What are people willing to pay to beat their disease? Five, ten million? But what about those who can't come up with that amount?"

Steiner's lips twist up in a sarcastic smirk. "They'll just

have to accept their fate or get some philanthropic organization to fund them. In any case, we get our money. As they say, 'no ticky, no laundry.'"

"Actually, I don't think anyone says that anymore," Steve says, rolling his eyes, "but I get your meaning. What if there is no cure after ten years, twenty years?"

"Again, just too bad for them. We're not making any promises or guarantees. Our only responsibility is that our patented drug will keep them in suspended animation for the length of time they want. The longer it is, the more we charge them. I already have our legal team drafting a detailed consent form that will shield us from liability." Steiner drains his glass then reaches for the bottle again. "And, Steve, have you thought about how we'll market it to healthy people who want to live in the future? You know, those who think they'll be able to take a trip to the moon or teleport to another city, or the ass-clown who expects to wake up and see world peace with all the nations' leaders sitting around singing Kumbaya?"

With that final remark, the two men burst out in laughter so loud it's heard not only by Steiner's secretary outside, but others in the adjoining second-floor offices, none of whom can fathom what has inspired their normally stoic CEO to such humor.

***

Throughout the week, Dr. Merriweather has been on the phone with George Irwin, the toxicologist at the Medical Examiner's Office. Each day, George has put him off, citing the difficulties in pinpointing the exact origin of the main agent in Saltzman's inhaler. Each day, he promises results "soon," only to give the same evasive response.

Friday morning, Dr. Merriweather and Dr. Glanville are with a patient when Merriweather's cell phone rings with a call from Mishy.

"Sorry to bother you, Chief, but you said to let you know if Dr. Irvin calls."

"Yes, thank you, Mishy, please have him hold. I'm on my way." Then, muttering an excuse about an urgent call, he tells Dr. Glanville to finish up the examination. "I'll be back as soon as I can," he says as he rushes from the room. Normally, he would never leave a patient so abruptly, but there is no way he's going to miss Irvin's call, not when it might help him figure out what had happened to Dr. Montel.

Three minutes later, he reaches his office and tells Mishy to put the call through.

"Okay, George, what've you got for me?"

"One hell of a potent poison," Irvin replies. "And actually it's similar to the tetrodotoxin you gave me last week from your voodoo-loving Haitian. The reason this took me so long is that it's the tetrodotoxin from the Pacific Puffer fish, which is slightly different chemically and much more potent than that found in the Caribbean-Atlantic species. What's more, the stuff in the inhaler is from the *poison glands* themselves. The poison is much more concentrated than the Haitian man's potion, which came from the fish's skin."

Merriweather pauses a moment, trying to digest the new information. "Holy crap, George. I really don't know what to make of this."

"That's just the beginning."

"There's more?"

"You bet! I also found some ciguatera fish poison in there too. The ciguatera poison potentiates the effect of the tetrodotoxin from the puffer fish glands and makes its effects last longer. It's probably why your resident went into a coma or a catatonic state for two and a half days. No offense, Bob, but did you get this stuff from some deranged marine biologist? I mean, this is like Jacques Cousteau becomes the Joker."

Merriweather knows exactly what he's talking about. He had ciguatera once himself from eating a big grouper. It was pretty bad, and his symptoms were right out of the textbook. When he held something cold, it felt hot; when he held something hot, it felt cold. He also felt weak for months. Indeed, the toxin certainly affected both sensory nerves and motor nerves. He could also see where it would extend the effect of the puffer fish toxin.

"George," he says thoughtfully, "what if lionfish toxin was added?"

"Bob, you just hit on my big worry. It would make it last a whole lot longer and be much more profound. Lionfish toxin keeps sodium channels open for a heck of a long time."

"Oh my God, I really need to think about this. Thanks a million, George. Great work. I owe you one."

"No problem, Bob. Keep sending the weird stuff. It keeps me from getting bored."

For the first time in a nearly a week, Merriweather forgets about his troubles with Heather; however, his sadness is now replaced with dread and remorse. Is his friend Saltzman using the lionfish spines he gave him in the inhaler? And for what purpose? Could it be to extend the catatonic state induced by the inhaler Montel used?

***

"Can either of you tell me what's going on here?" asks Chief Russell.

She gestures to the small stack of photographs of Colonel Bradley leaving Dr. Saltzman's lab, as well as the report Detective Taft emailed Molinaro that morning.

Andy takes the lead. "We think Colonel Bradley is somehow involved with one of Saltzman's medical projects and that he reports about it to Apollo Drug Company. Issy researched registered research projects and found that Saltzman is developing a pain reliever, which would be business as usual if it weren't for Bradley's track record as a schemer and the cloak-and-dagger way he's acting."

Just then, Issy receives a text message from Dr. Merriweather: *Call me ASAP. Think I've figured out something about the zombie murders.*

"Merriweather has news."

"Okay, give him a call." Russell picks up the desk phone and hands it to her. "And put him on speaker so we can all hear it."

A moment later, Merriweather's voice fills the office. "Dr. Merriweather, this is Captain Jennifer Russell from the 16th District police station in Cutler Ridge. You're on speaker with Detectives Molinaro and Ruiz."

Merriweather utters a quick greeting to the three cops then says, "I think Dr. Jake Saltzman is somehow involved with the zombie murders."

"Go on, Doctor," replies Chief Russell.

After relating the episodes of Danny, Bevo St. Claire and David Montel, Merriweather moves on to the toxicology findings.

"So what does all this mean, Doctor?" Russell asks. "Can you tie it together?"

"Well, Issy told me that you have four zombies and that they're big. Dr. Saltzman is doing some supposed sleep study on four former football players—two black, two white. Doesn't that fit the descriptions of the zombies?"

"Yes, it does. Go on."

"Well, the two toxins found in Dr. Saltzman's inhaler

turned my own resident into a zombie. Three puffs resulted in his falling into some sort of trance followed by aggression—which, from what I'm told, was triggered by the flash of a cell phone camera—and finally, coma. It's all a matter of nerve physiology. The puffer fish toxin opens sodium channels in the brain, discharging nerve cells. The brain goes numb, if you can call it that, but ready to spring into action by a startling event which causes tissues to release sodium and turn at least parts of the brain into some type of hyper function. The ciguatera fish poison coupled with lionfish toxin was Saltzman's attempt to make the pain relief you get from his combination last longer, only it had unintended side effects."

"Wow, Dr. Merriweather, that's a pretty involved scenario. And you say these zombie guys are now in Saltzman's lab?"

"Yes, according to Luke Young, my resident on station there. They're in beds in a sleep lab, supposedly being treated for chronic pain from football injuries. Luke's the one that got you the DNA samples from each of them—the ones you connected to the murderers at the Miami River Diner." Merriweather pauses. "Chief Russel, I'm concerned that it may be even worse than that and that I may have contributed to it."

Russell laughs humorlessly. "Four zombies terrorizing the city, how much worse can it get? And how did you contribute to this mess?"

"Well, I gave lionfish spines to Dr. Saltzman, the same ones that caused the pain and the zombie-like state in Danny, the dockhand I told you about. If ciguatera fish poison extends the zombie effect of the puffer fish toxin for two to three days, lionfish toxin will likely extend it much further—possibly months or even years. Worse of all, the violent behavior triggered when the person is startled will be very much heightened and longer lasting if lionfish toxin is added to this witch's brew."

"From what you say, Doctor, we need to pay a visit to Dr. Saltzman right away."

Merriweather sighs sadly. "I know you have to, but let me talk to him first. It's hard for me to accept that this brilliant man dedicated to curing pain would have any malicious intent. Maybe I can make him come to his senses."

"Okay, Dr. Merriweather, we'll give you until ten a.m. tomorrow, then we'll be there with a search warrant and a swat team."

"Deal. I'll get there early."

CHAPTER 25
First, Do No Harm

At six o'clock Saturday morning, David Steiner and Steve Bloom leave the Intercontinental Hotel on Biscayne Boulevard where they registered yesterday evening under fictitious names and phony IDs. They are greeted curbside by an Apollo Miami drug representative for the short drive to Dr. Saltzman's lab, as a cab would have a record of their trip. The same is true of the security cameras at the Life Sciences entrance, which they have asked Saltzman to disable.

Although he thinks his benefactors are a bit paranoid, he happily complies with their requests. It is two weeks into the experiment, and everything is going as well as they could have hoped. The four subjects are still in a state of suspended animation with stable life signs and no apparent clinical or cellular signs of aging. After the usual pleasantries, Dr. Saltzman goes over the planned re-dosing tasks.

"Gentlemen, as you can see, we've achieved two weeks of complete suspended animation. From my calculations, the initial dose should last for six months, where upon re-dosing will be necessary. However, since every patient is of a different weight, the time and amount to re-dose will be different for each subject. To accommodate this, I have developed an infrared retinal scanner which will measure the blood concentration of each of my three main agents. From this information, the computer in the control panel will trigger the precise amount for re-dosing when the concentrations fall below the levels I have programmed."

"How is the re-dosing actually carried out, Doctor?" asks David Steiner.

"Simple! The computer will signal this robotic arm to move to the patient's mouth and nose, where a vaporized form of my agents is allowed to cloud over the area while the retinal scanner continues to measure the blood concentration of the agents. When the blood levels reach that which will ensure another three months, six months, nine months or more of suspended animation, a feedback signal withdraws the vaporizing device."

Colonel Bradley nods slowly in genuine appreciation. "Very good, Dr. Saltzman, very good!"

David Steiner and Steve Bloom look at each other with a look of awe. Clearly, they invested in the right guy.

Just then, several loud knocks are heard all the way from the locked reception room door.

"Jake—Jake, open up, it's Bob Merriweather."

Saltzman freezes where he stands, his eyes darting fearfully among his three conspirators.

"C'mon, Jake, I know you're in there. I saw your car parked out front." Merriweather sighs. "We have to talk, now. I know what you're doing."

"What the hell is this?" Steiner whispers. "You promised you wouldn't say anything."

"I didn't!" Saltzman whines. "But I know Bob Merriweather, and he won't go away. I have to answer it."

"Okay," Steiner snaps, "but you better not let him know we're here. Get rid of him as fast as you can."

Jake Saltzman nods then slips out the lab door, closing it behind him. He then goes through his own office and out into the reception area. Then, adopting a smile, he booms, "Bob! What're you doing here on Saturday morning?"

Merriweather eyes him suspiciously. "Why don't we go sit in your office?"

"Calm down, Bob," Saltzman says, his smile in place. "I'm in the middle of a research project here. We're just going through some chronic pain elimination studies with several patients. We can't disturb the treatment session now."

"Jake, that's a bunch of bullshit. I know about the former high school football players in there." Merriweather pauses. "I also know that they are the so-called zombie murderers."

"That's preposterous!" Saltzman explodes, partly in fear and partly in genuine indignation at being questioned by a friend. "I'm only treating the pain from their football injuries. I can assure you, these boys are not murderers, just patients."

"Oh yeah? Then how do you explain the DNA swab from two of them that matches the DNA left at the murder scene at the diner?"

DNA match? There's been no such detail in the media. "But—but how did you get DNA samples from them?" Saltzman asks, the color draining from his face.

"That doesn't matter, Jake. What you're doing is unethical and wrong."

Now cornered, Saltzman tries to reason with his old friend. "Bob, do you remember the Star Trek episodes we watched while on call? Do you remember their credo? That 'the needs of the many outweigh the needs of the few'? It's the same here. These four individuals will go down in history as the first to experience human suspended animation. Think of what this means! People can wake up in the future when other groundbreaking developments are able to cure their now incurable diseases. Not only that, it'll make long-distance space travel a reality and possibly allow us to colonize other planets."

Merriweather shakes his head, unable to believe what he is hearing. "Jake, you're wrong. That's not outweighing the needs of the few. These four individuals will realize no need to be outweighed. You're not curing their pain. You're misleading them. They can't sleep their lives away. In doing so, you're denying them the rehab program that can really help their football careers get back on track. Look at what that kind of rehab did for the former UM football star, Willis McGehee. He became an All-Pro." Merriweather's tone softens. "That credo was made for television. The real credo, the only one that matters to us, is that of Plato: 'First do no harm.' Jake, you're doing harm to them. If turning people into zombies is a side effect of your treatment, it also harms the many. I'm begging you, Jake, come to your senses before it's too late."

While the two doctors continue their debate over medical progress versus morality and professional ethics, Saltzman's visitors take the opportunity to study the monitors more closely. They approach the four subjects, lying quietly in their respective beds with eyes half open, and touch their skin.

"They feel warm," notes Colonel Bradley. He then waves his hand in front of John Malnicki's eyes to perhaps elicit a blink. No such blink occurs. He looks at Dave Steiner and the drug rep, now standing by Reginald Doyo, and says, "They truly are in suspended animation. It's not just a theory, it's a reality. Saltzman is amazing. He's truly amazing."

Steve Bloom has a more practical reaction. "Dave, we need to get his formula patented. What do you think about making him director of Advanced Research at Apollo Pharmaceuticals? If we make him an official employee, the patent will be legally ours. And Saltzman is more likely to stay with us throughout the implementation phase, not to mention the kudos Apollo will receive when he's awarded the Nobel Prize in Medicine for our drug."

"Steve, I like you're thinking," Steiner says, pulling out his phone and pointing in Reggie's direction. "Now, you and the Colonel move next to that guy and his monitors. I'll get some pictures, then you take some of me next to the others. They'll be historical pictures for sure."

The two men comply, and David Steiner positions his phone at the best possible angle. A second later, the flash, which is needed in the subdued lighting of Saltzman's lab, goes off. Steve Bloom returns the favor with his own cell phone, emitting a second flash. None of them notice the eyes of all four subjects widening. Slowly, each one comes to a semiconscious state, becoming aware of lying in a bed and, more importantly, the uncomfortable sensation in their penises from the urinary catheters. Almost in unison, they pull them out and, in doing so, cause a shock of an acute strange stimulation coursing through their loins as the balloon at the end of the catheter expands the urethra tenfold. To the shock of Colonel Bradley and the three men from Apollo, all four arise out of their beds, each with the blank, straight-ahead stare described at the murder scenes. John Malnicki grabs Colonel Bradley before he can escape, while the gaze of the other three fixate on Steiner, Steve Bloom and the drug rep who are now clawing at the door to Saltzman's office. Oblivious to Bradley's screams, Steiner fumbles with the door lock.

Meanwhile, Bradley struggles to get loose of the death grip around his neck. Despite being a fit and trained ex-marine, he is no match for the "zombie's" strength. John Malnicki squeezes down on the Colonel's throat, crushing his larynx. With eyes bulging and a bloody froth emerging from his nostrils and mouth, Colonel Bradley becomes the eighth victim of the zombie murders.

Hearing the commotion, Merriweather and Saltzman break off their debate and enter Saltzman's office, where they find the terrified Steiner and Bloom. With shaking voices, the two men explain that the four subjects emerged from their suspended animation and were acting strange—strange enough to suspect that Colonel Bradley's life is in peril. Then, without another word, they quickly run out of Saltzman's lab and through the doors of the Life Sciences Building before anyone else learns of their presence.

Merriweather turns to his friend. "Jake, don't you see? These four guys are the zombie murderers. The puffer fish toxins together with the ciguatera and lionfish toxins have deadly, unintended side effects, one of which is near-superhuman strength. They don't realize what they're doing and don't remember any of it later. We have to do something. The detectives and an entire SWAT team will be here any minute. You know they'll just kill all four of them. These guys are innocent. What they did and are now doing is caused by your drug combination. Don't you believe me now?"

Finally, the truth of what Merriweather is saying penetrates Saltzman's defenses. He grips a chair and slowly lowers himself into it. "Oh God, Bob! What have I done? I never meant for this to happen. I really didn't know that they were the ones in the newspapers. All right, all right, but what can we do now?"

"Jake, do you remember those old movies we used to watch in between patients during those late nights on call? Remember how they would put people to sleep with the old ether on the handkerchief trick?"

Saltzman immediately follows Merriweather's train of thought. "Yeah, I do. You know I have some sevoforane anesthetic in the cupboard above my desk here and lab towels in my drawer...."

As they are planning their strategy, they hear noises coming from the lobby. Dr. Merriweather glances at his watch and groans just as Andy and Issy come through the door. They are followed by Chief Russell and at least twelve fully armored and weapon-toting SWAT team members.

"Chief Russell, I need you to hold off the SWAT team for now. The zombies are loose in Saltzman's lab, but it turns out they're innocent in all this; they only killed people while under the influence of some experimental drugs."

Russell pauses for a beat. "I appreciate all your help with this case, Dr. Merriweather, but the safety of the community is our largest concern here."

"I understand, but give me and Dr. Saltzman a chance first. Please."

"Are they confined to the lab?"

"They are."

"Okay, you have ten minutes, then the SWAT team goes in." She pauses again. "I'm assuming you have a plan, Doctor?"

"Yes, of course. We put them under a general anesthetic with this sevoforane anesthetic agent. It's what is used in almost every OR surgery today. We get them to the hospital. You can keep them shackled while Dr. Saltzman oversees their weaning off of the drugs that turned them into zombies in the first place."

"And how are you going to administer these anesthetics? Zombies usually don't hold still for such things."

"We soak these towels in the anesthetic, position ourselves behind each one and cover their mouth and nose then hold on."

"Like an old movie? Sorry, Doctor Merriweather, but that sounds crazy."

Jake Saltzman breaks in. "I can assure you it'll work. The coefficient of solubility is so high, they'll be under in less than five seconds. This is all my fault. I have to make it right."

Russell sighs. "Okay, but if it doesn't work, we're doing it my way."

A second later, Andy Molinaro and Issy Ruiz volunteer to help, and Dr. Merriweather quickly lays out the plan.

"We soak these towels in the sevo until they're almost dripping. Keep it away from your own mouth and nose. I don't want you sleeping on the job."

Issy gives him a wry smile. "Corny as ever, huh, Chief?"

"When we go in," he continues, "I'll take the larger of the two black guys. Andy, you take the taller, muscular black guy. Jake, you take the biggest white guy, and, Issy, you take the other white guy. We go in calmly without saying a word. When we're all maneuvered behind our targets,

Andy, you give us the signal, then quickly place your right hand holding the towels firmly over their mouths and noses, and hang on, okay?"

They nod then move quietly toward the door to the lab.

When they open the door, the first thing they notice is that all four zombies are standing apart from each other and facing in different directions, making it easier to approach them from behind. The second thing they see is Colonel Bradley's body lying on the floor by John Malnicki's bed. With his eyes bulged and tongue protruding grossly from the corner of his mouth, he serves as a warning of what can happen to them if they fail.

Once everyone is in position, Andy gives the signal and is the first to pounce on his target, Reginald Doyo. The others do the same, with Merriweather on Big Cat Thompson, Saltzman on John Malnicki and Issy on the quarterback Charlie Harper. The rapidly acting sevoforane in its high concentration in the soaked towels, coupled with the inhalation reflex of being startled, works as predicted. However, before going under, John Malnicki is able to shake off Jake Saltzman. His gaze fixates on the doctor, and he lets out a low snarl. As he is about to seize him, Andy grabs him by the neck and places the towel over his mouth. With Andy's firm hold, the second administration of the potent anesthetic does the trick, and John Malnicki finally goes limp and is guided to the floor.

In all the commotion, no one notices as the rest of the Apollo team quietly exits the room, then the building. Within minutes, they are headed to the airport, relieved but shaken to the core.

With the zombies now truly unconscious, Dr. Saltzman and Dr. Merriweather suddenly find themselves reliving their residency. Enlisting Andy and Issy's help, they intubate each of the four young men and assist their respirations with ambu bags, then await the paramedics who will transport them to the main Dade County Medical ICU. Though the zombies are anesthetized, the SWAT team handcuffs each one, as well as Dr. Saltzman. Merriweather watches, truly saddened, as Chief Russell steps toward his old friend.

"Dr. Saltzman, you're under arrest as an accessory to murder, kidnapping, and depraved indifference. You have the right to remain silent. Anything you say can and will be used against you in a court of law. You have the right to an attorney. If you can't afford an attorney, one will be provided for you. Do you understand, Doctor?"

Saltzman seems to age ten years as his watery eyes flick from Russell to Merriweather.

"Yes," he manages, "I do."

The ambulances pull up just as Russell escorts Dr. Saltzman out of the building. They are followed seconds later by C.C. Murphy.

Andy and Issy look at each other in astonishment. "Now how in God's name did that woman get here so fast?"

"I don't know, Andy," Chief Russell says, "but I'm going to deal with her right now." She turns to face the advancing reporter. "Ms. Murphy, right on time. You can report that the zombie murders have been solved and that the suspects are in custody, thanks to the hard work of the 'glamour detectives' you've been criticizing over the past three weeks. Be sure to put that into your next column, won't you?"

CHAPTER 26
Fake News and a Dose of Reality

That evening finds Dr. Merriweather sitting in front of his television gently petting his white Labrador retriever Tubby and sipping on Amarula, the only liquor he cares to drink. Amarula is a cream liquor made from the Amarula fruit in South Africa and tastes similar to the Bailey's cream liquor more common in the United States. He was first introduced to it on his first of many photographic safaris to South Africa. Maybe it was taking in the incredible sunset with Heather, or perhaps it was just the cute but unconfirmed stories of elephants careening around drunk from eating decaying Amarula fruit that got him started on it. Since then, he's always found it relaxing. Tonight, though, even his favorite drink brings up his recent romantic troubles.

He sighs as he recalls the earlier events of the day, particularly the realization that his good friend was the mastermind behind the zombie murders and that he himself unknowingly contributed to the zombie concoction. Ironically, it was this contribution that also led him to help crack the case; at least Robert can take solace in that.

Just then, a Channel 5 news promo gets his attention.

"Today," announces anchor Pedro Suarez, "you'll hear how the zombie murderers were finally brought to justice and who was really behind these horrific crimes. We'll also bring you an exclusive interview with Miami Tribune News Reporter Catherine Murphy, who has been following this story from its inception. We'll be back after these messages."

Robert patiently waits through several commercials, only to be frustrated when several other news stories are parceled in before the report on the zombie murders. Finally, anchorman Suarez begins:

"Now, with the zombie murderers in custody, the community can breathe a sigh of relief. It seems that four young men turned out to be the so-called zombies. It also seems eight victims succumbed to these four before Chief of Police Jennifer Russell put the handcuffs on them just a few hours ago. The motive for the killing spree is still unknown, but perhaps Catherine Murphy can give our viewers some insight … Catherine."

"Yes, Pedro. I have learned that the four young men were part of an illicit drug experiment gone out of control. It befuddled the two detectives working on the case far too long. However, it was eventually exposed by oral and maxillofacial surgery resident Dr. Luke Young, who provided the evidence that a rogue researcher was behind it all." C.C. pauses for effect. "But, Pedro, I believe a celebration is premature. We don't have the name of this researcher as of yet, and we don't know the extent of his illicit research. Who knows, there may even be more zombies out there? Look how long it took the glamor detectives to track down these four. We should all still be nervous."

"Thank you, Catherine. And now, the weather with Ryan West."

Dr. Merriweather takes a sip of Amarula and looks at his dog.

"Well, Tubby, it wasn't exactly 'fake news', but it's pretty close. That woman wants some news reporting prize at the expense of public fear and panic. She has no idea of what really went into solving these crimes. So much for investigative reporting, actually reporting the complete truth."

Tubby just looks up at him and wags his tail.

Dr. Merriweather turns off the television, and, but for the panting of his three dogs, the room fills with a lonely silence. His thoughts turn to Heather, and he is once again gripped with an uncharacteristic and most uncomfortable indecisiveness. He has left her several messages over the past week, not one of which has been answered. Should he call just one more time, or write her off as his failed last chance for a meaningful relationship? Part of him wants to let it go just so he could begin to remove Heather from his mind, if not his heart, but something inside him makes him pick up the phone. To his surprise, she answers on the first ring.

"Well, you finally called."

Robert presses the phone more tightly to his ear, as if this will help him better discern her tone.

"Heather, I've called you nearly every day this week!"

"You did? Hold on a minute."

A moment later she returns. "Oh, Robert, I'm sorry. I'm just now seeing the voicemails from you. I was at a book convention, and there was no cell phone service in the venue. Then, every evening, I had to go out to dinners with prospective book authors and advertisers for our journals, and…" Her voice trails off.

"And … your work situation caused you to ignore me just like mine caused me to ignore you."

She sighs. "Yes, yes, it did. I'm sorry, Bob, not for being upset that you forgot our weekend, but for the way I spoke to you that night. You didn't deserve that. I guess I was just feeling … scared."

Merriweather draws back in surprise. "Scared? Of what?"

"That I was losing you…" she says quietly.

"The way my ex-wife did," he finishes. "I'm sorry you felt that way, and I promise, you couldn't lose me if you tried." He chuckles. "Look, I thought you were ignoring my calls all week, and I still tried again."

She laughs too. "So, is that your version of romance?"

"Actually, it is. I'm a scientist and not very good at charming phrases and love sonnets, but you know my deep feelings for you. If we are the mature professionals we think we are, we can work out the distractions and distance between us. Look at your schedule, and come down as soon as you can. We'll make up for lost time."

"Okay," she says, and Robert detects an odd note in her voice.

"Heather, are we okay now?"

"Yes, of course we are. Goodbye, Robert. I'll call you tomorrow."

As they end the call, Robert is smiling and anticipating the first good night's sleep in a week. *Everything is fine,* he tells himself as he shuts the TV and brings his empty glass to the sink. It's not until he slides into bed that he realizes he never once in their makeup phone call told Heather he loved her. He also realizes that those words were all she really wanted to hear.

That's what I heard in her voice, he tells himself, disappointed.

CHAPTER 27
Epilogue—The Future

Six weeks after the murder of Chester Bland that started the bizarre sequence of events, and three weeks after its equally bizarre conclusion in Saltzman's lab, the four high school football stars are already making progress in the University of Miami Sports Medicine Rehab Center. Though there has not yet been an official determination about their legal fate, the general consensus among their lawyers and talking heads in the media is that they will be treated not as perpetrators but as victims of Saltzman's experiment. In the meantime, they remain focused on joining the UM football program and getting back to life as relatively career-oriented twenty-somethings.

Doctor Saltzman's future is far less optimistic. His lawyer's argument that he should be shown leniency, given his lifelong dedication to science and his assistance in controlling his zombie creations at the end, will likely hold little weight in the face of the horrible crimes he caused. For Saltzman, however, even the prospect of spending the rest of his life in jail pales in comparison to the sentence he's already received: the revocation of his medical license and his discrediting in the scientific medical world.

For the Miami Police Department, particularly Chief Jennifer Russell's squad, the mood is nothing short of jubilant. Detectives Molinaro and Ruiz have received meritorious service awards for solving the case and ending the panic over the now notorious "zombie murders."

For Dr. Merriweather, the awards Issy is receiving as a detective is especially poignant, though not surprising. In the years she worked for him, he came to know her as someone who would excel at whatever she put her mind to, whether it was managing his hectic schedule or unearthing an evil plot to turn young men to zombies. Indeed, he is grinning broadly as he walks into a subdued but pleasant gathering honoring the detectives at Mayor Ecchavaria's office. However, as he moves through the crowd offering his congratulations, there is another, more personal reason for his high spirits: Heather is on his arm.

With a Cuban coffee in hand the mayor begins. "Detectives, I can't over-emphasize the gratitude the citizens of Miami have for you. There was a time when I myself thought these murders would never be solved." He raises his coffee toward Merriweather. "Dr. Merriweather, I understand your efforts and knowledge were critical to solving this case as well. I also understand that this victory came at some personal cost to you."

Robert becomes more subdued as he addresses the small crowd. "Thank you, Mr. Mayor. And yes, while I'm relieved that this case has been solved, I am truly saddened that such a good friend and a brilliant, well-meaning man came to such an end. However, like all of us..." Merriweather pauses for a beat to give Heather a pointed look, "...he had flaws, in this case an obsession with recognition. I can only hope that his pioneering work on opening sodium channels in the brain can lead to many new discoveries by researchers that follow him. It's the breakthrough for which he ironically will not be credited."

"We understand," the Mayor says. "I've heard that there were others involved in this plot along with Dr. Saltzman." He glances over at Jennifer Russell for confirmation. "Is this true?"

She nods then gestures for Dr. Merriweather to continue.

"Yes. We have since learned that David Steiner, CEO of Apollo Pharmaceuticals was involved. Steiner and an Apollo drug rep were in the lab the day we subdued the four young men. Apparently, Apollo bank-rolled Saltzman's work on this project, motivated of course by the potential billions in revenue a discovery of this magnitude could have generated. In fact, I believe it was their influence and deep pockets that enticed my colleague to step beyond ethical boundaries. It seems this zombie thing was a perfect storm of narcissism, greed, and weird science."

"I tend to agree with you, especially after everything I've heard about Dr. Saltzman." The mayor smiles. "I also understand that you've had run-ins with Apollo before." He then turns to Chief Russell. "Anything to add, Jennifer?"

"Yes," she says, turning to Andy and Issy. "Detectives, this is your day. In the face of a seemingly unsolvable case, and very unfavorable media coverage, you proved yourselves to be truly exceptional detectives. And on that note, I'm *officially* making an exception to the rule that partners cannot be involved in a relationship. Are you okay with that, Mr. Mayor?"

Everyone turns to Ecchavaria, who replies, "Of course, Chief Russell. Today of all days, how can I refuse you?"

Heather squeezes Merriweather's hand affectionately. "Just like I can't refuse you."

He smiles. "Excuse me a minute. I want to take a picture of something I saw outside the mayor's office." With that, he slips away, leaving Heather and several others exchanging quizzical glances.

True to his word, he returns a moment later. "Sorry about that. I just wanted to show Heather a picture of something interesting." He brings up the image on his phone and hands it to her. Thinking Robert's actions are a little out of place during a party, she gives the screen a casual glance and at first doesn't recognize what she sees. A second later, her eyes widen and return to the image of an open jewelry box with a diamond ring in it and a little note reading *Marry me?*

As the awkward proposal sinks in, she looks up at Robert and blurts out, "YES!" then pulls him into a hug. "I thought you said you're not a romantic?"

A moment later, the couple turns to find the others staring at them with knowing smiles.

"You knew?" Heather exclaims.

"You know how proper the Chief is," Issy says, smiling. "He wanted to make sure he wasn't stealing our thunder. Anyway, I had a hard time keeping it from Andy."

"You had a hard time keeping it from everyone," Andy adds, earning a good-natured elbow from his partner. "Congratulations, you two."

"I'm just glad C.C. Murphy isn't here," Chief Russell adds, "and a bit surprised she's not hounding us for details."

"Oh, she did," announces Issy, "but I took care of it."

"You did?" the others say in unison. "How?"

"Well, after being so critical in her coverage of the case, she didn't have the guts to face me in person, but she did text me asking for an exclusive 'just between us girls.' This was my response." Issy takes out her cell phone and holds it up for the others to see.

"Sorry, C.C., but such a request must go through the mayor's executive secretary Helen Waite for approval. I suggest you go to Helen Waite."

Amidst the puzzled looks of those wondering who Ms. Waite is, Heather starts laughing.

"Go to," she says slowly as she glances at the others, "hell … and … wait."

Merriweather leans over and places a kiss on her cheek.

"Ladies and gentlemen," he says with a sweeping gesture, "this is why she'll be my bride!"

And with that, the room erupts in laughter.

About the Author

Doctor Robert Marx is one of the world's most predominant stem cell researchers and bone marrow transplant specialists, and he has now written two bone-chilling fiction novels that are so compelling, it blurs the line of imagination and reality.

Professor of Surgery and Chief of the Division of Oral and Maxillofacial Surgery at the University of Miami Miller School of Medicine, Dr. Marx is well known as an educator, researcher, and innovative surgeon.

He has pioneered new concepts and treatments for pathologies of the oral and facial area as well as new techniques in reconstructive surgery.